the White giraffe

the White giraffe

LAUREN St. JOHN

illustrated by David Dean

Dial Books for Young Readers / Walden Media

DIAL BOOKS FOR YOUNG READERS
A division of Penguin Young Readers Group
Published by The Penguin Group
Penguin Group (USA) Inc., 375 Hudson Street, New York, NY 10014, U.S.A.
Penguin Group (Canada), 90 Eglinton Avenue East, Suite 700, Toronto, Ontario, Canada M4P
2Y3 (a division of Pearson Penguin Canada Inc.) • Penguin Books Ltd, 80 Strand, London
WC2R 0RL, England • Penguin Ireland, 25 St. Stephen's Green, Dublin 2, Ireland (a division of
Penguin Books Ltd) • Penguin Group (Australia), 250 Camberwell Road, Camberwell, Victoria
3124, Australia (a division of Pearson Australia Group Pty Ltd) • Penguin Books India Pvt Ltd,
11 Community Centre, Panchsheel Park, New Delhi - 110 017, India • Penguin Group (NZ), Cnr
Airborne and Rosedale Roads, Albany, Auckland 1310, New Zealand (a division of Pearson New
Zealand Ltd) • Penguin Books (South Africa) (Pty) Ltd, 24 Sturdee Avenue, Rosebank, Johannesburg 2196, South Africa • Penguin Books Ltd, Registered Offices: 80 Strand, London WC2R
0RL, England

This book is published in partnership with Walden Media, LLC. Walden Media and the
Walden Media skipping stone logo are trademarks and registered trademarks of Walden
Media, LLC, 294 Washington Street, Boston, Massachusetts 02108.

First published in the United States 2007 by Dial Books for Young Readers
Published in Great Britain 2006 by Orion Children's Books
Text copyright © 2006 by Lauren St. John
Illustrations copyright © 2006 by David Dean

Designed by Nancy R. Leo-Kelly
Text set in Miller Text • Printed in the U.S.A.
1 3 5 7 9 10 8 6 4 2

Library of Congress Cataloging-in-Publication Data
St. John, Lauren, date.
The white giraffe / Lauren St. John ; illustrated by David Dean.
p. cm.
Summary: After a fire kills her parents, eleven-year-old Martine must leave England
to live with her grandmother on a wildlife game reserve in South Africa,
where she befriends a mythical white giraffe.
ISBN 978-0-8037-3211-7
[1. Animals, Mythical—Fiction. 2. Giraffe—Fiction. 3. Orphans—Fiction.
4. Game reserves—Fiction. 5. Wildlife conservation—Fiction. 6. South Africa—Fiction.]
I. Dean, David, date, ill. II. Title.
PZ7.S77435Wh 2007 [Fic]—dc22 2006021323

*For Sophie, aged 10,
who, like me,
loves horses and shy giraffes*

1

People like to say that things come in threes, but the way Martine looked at it, that all depends on when you start counting and when you stop. For instance, she could say that one bad thing happened along with three good things, but the truth was that the one bad thing was the very worst thing in the whole world, another was so small she didn't really notice it at the time, and something else that she first thought was bad luck later turned out to be the best kind of fortune anyone could wish for. Whichever way you added it up, though, one thing was certain. The night Martine Allen turned eleven years old was the night her life changed completely and was never the same again.

It was New Year's Eve. At the time, Martine was asleep in bed and she was dreaming about a place she'd never been to before. The reason she was so positive was because it was too beautiful ever to forget. As far as the eye could see, there were lawns lined with exotic flowers and trees. Behind them, rising into a clear sky, was a mountain made majestic by granite cliffs and lush green forests. Children were laughing and chasing moths through beds of dusky-pink flowers and, in the distance, Martine could hear drums and soaring voices. But for some reason she felt apprehensive. Dread prickled her skin.

All at once, the sky began to boil with a turbulent violet light and a thick tablecloth of steel-gray cloud raced down the mountain. The day turned from sunny to sinister in seconds. Then one of the children shouted, "Hey, look what I found!"

It was a wild goose with a broken wing. But instead of helping it, some of the children began tormenting it. Martine, who could never bear to see any creature hurt, tried to stop them, but in the dream they turned on her instead. Next thing she knew she was on the ground crying and the injured bird was in her arms.

Then something very peculiar happened. Her hands, holding the wild goose, heated up to the point where they were practically glowing, and electricity crackled through her. She saw, in a swirl of smoke, black men in horned antelope masks and rhinoceroses breathing fire, and heard voices as old as Time. She knew they wanted to speak to her, but she couldn't hear what they were saying. Suddenly, the bird stirred. Martine opened her palms and it shook out its wings and flew into the violet sky.

In the dream, she looked up smiling, but the other children didn't smile back. They stared at her with a mixture of horror and disbelief. "Witch," they chanted, "witch, witch, witch," and they began to chase her. Martine fled sobbing up the mountain, into a dark forest. But her legs were unimaginably heavy, hooked thorns tore at her ankles, and she was losing her way in the cloud. And all the while it was getting hotter and hotter. Then a hand grabbed her and she began to scream and scream and scream.

It was the sound of her own screams that finally woke Martine. She shot up in bed. It was pitch dark and it took a few seconds for her to realize she'd been asleep. None of it had happened. There was no mountain and no bird. She was safely in her bed in Hampshire, England, with her parents sleeping soundly across the corridor. Heart pounding, she sank back into the pillows. She was a bit dizzy and she still felt very, very hot.

Hot? How could it possibly be *hot?* It was midwinter. Martine's eyes flew open. Something was wrong. Frantically she fumbled for the bedside lamp, but for some reason it wasn't working. She sat up again. An orange light was flickering beneath the bedroom door and gray ribbons of smoke were drifting up from it.

"Fire!" yelled Martine. "Fire!"

She leaped out of bed, caught her foot in the blankets, and crashed to the ground. Tears of panic sprang into her eyes. She wiped them away roughly. If I don't think clearly, she told herself, I'll never get out alive. The corner of the door turned molten red and broke away, and a plume of smoke poured in after it. Martine began coughing violently. She clawed at the floor for yesterday's sweatshirt, discarded there when she put on her pajamas. Almost cheering with thankfulness when she found it immediately, she tied it around her face. Then she scrambled to her feet, heaved up the window, and leaned out into the starless night. What was she supposed to do? *Jump?*

Martine stood paralyzed with terror. Far below her, the snow glinted mockingly in the darkness. Behind her, the room was filling with smoke and fumes, and the fire was roaring like a factory furnace. It was blisteringly, murderously hot—so hot that she felt as if her pajamas were melting off her back. The window was the only way out. Swinging her legs over the sill, she reached out and grabbed a clump of ivy. It was as wet as lettuce and came away in her hand. Martine almost toppled after it. She tried again, this time knocking away the packed snow and groping behind the vine for a pipe or a crevice or anything at all that would give her a handhold. Nothing!

Martine's eyes streamed. Moments remained between her and disaster, but she jumped back into the room, snatched the sheets off the bed, and knotted them together, tying one end to the bed leg nearest the window. There was no time to test it. She just had to hope that it would hold. As fast as she dared, she climbed out of the window, clinging to the sheet-rope with both hands. She knew very well that it wouldn't reach the ground, but it might get her a little closer.

She was still high in the air when her hands, stiff as frozen fish sticks in the gusting Arctic wind, lost their grip and she crashed into the snow. Martine dragged herself upright, shivering, and hobbled along the side of the house to the front, but as soon as she rounded the corner, she no longer thought about that. She was too busy taking in the appalling scene before her. Her home was a raging inferno. Flames leaped in every window and coils of smoke billowed into the night sky. A crowd had gathered on the lawn and all along the street, doors were opening and more people were rushing to join them. Sirens announced the rapid approach of the fire department.

"Mum! Dad!" yelled Martine, and she ran around the side to the front of the house.

Shocked faces turned in her direction. There was a collective gasp. The Allens' elderly next-door neighbor opened her mouth when she saw Martine rushing across the lawn, but no sound came out. Mr. and Mrs. Morrison, who lived farther up the street, were also rooted to the spot, but Mr. Morrison, a burly former rugby player, shook himself into action at the last moment and managed to catch Martine as she flew by.

"Let me go," sobbed Martine, but even as she spoke she

knew it was too late. The walls of the house were collapsing in a molten heap. Within minutes, there was nothing left. The fire department had arrived, but the most they could do was put the flames out.

Mrs. Morrison put her arms around Martine and held her tightly. "I'm so sorry, my dear," she said. "I'm so sorry." Others came over to console her, and Mr. Morrison gave her his coat to put on over her pajamas.

Through the screen of Martine's tears, the still-glowing embers and bubbles of the firemen's foam shone like rubies and diamonds in the fading night. Only a few hours ago, she'd been enjoying a birthday dinner with her parents. They'd made pancakes and filled them with almonds, bananas, and melted chocolate and shaped them into cones they could eat with their hands. Martine and her mum had laughed at her dad, David, who was talking so much that he hadn't noticed that his pancake was leaking chocolate down his shirt. Only one thing had happened that Martine now thought strange.

They'd been on their way up to bed. Martine's mum had kissed her and gone on ahead and Martine was walking up the stairs with her dad. When they reached her bedroom door, he hugged her good night, ruffled her hair, and told her he loved her, just as he always did. But then—almost as if he sensed something was going to happen—he said something odd.

"You have to trust, Martine. Everything happens for a reason."

And Martine had smiled at him and thought how lovely

6

her parents were even if they were sometimes a little weird, and she'd gone into her room, not knowing that they were the last words he would ever say to her.

Not knowing she would never see either of her parents again.

2

It was Mr. Grice from Social Services who told Martine that she would be moving to Africa. Cape Town, South Africa, to be precise.

"*South Africa!*" cried Martine. "Why South Africa?"

"Well," said Mr. Grice, "it seems that your only surviving relative is, in fact, living on a game reserve in South Africa. A Mrs. Gwyn Thomas, who, I'm told, is your grandmother."

Martine was stunned. "I don't have a grandmother," she said slowly.

Mr. Grice frowned. He reached into his pocket for his glasses and consulted his file again. "No, I assure you there's no mistake. I have her letter here."

8

He handed Martine a sheet of cream writing paper.

Dear Mr. Grice,

Thank you for your condolences on the sad loss of my daughter, Veronica Allen, and her husband, David, two of the finest people I have ever known. I was unaware that my daughter had stipulated that I should have guardianship of their child, Martine, if anything ever happened to her. However, I will accept the responsibility. It is the least I can do. I enclose an airplane ticket to Cape Town and £150 for the girl's expenses. I rarely go into the city and would be grateful if you could ensure that she is adequately clothed for the South African weather.

Yours truly,
Gwyn Thomas

There was something about the tone of the letter that bothered Martine. Her grandmother didn't seem at all enthusiastic about the prospect of taking her on. Quite the reverse. From the sound of things, she expected Martine to be a burden. She couldn't even face the prospect of buying her a few summer clothes. She had clearly adored Martine's parents, but that didn't mean she wanted to be stuck with Martine. And what about her grandfather? There was no mention of him.

Martine handed the letter back to Mr. Grice. "I'm not

going," she said. "She doesn't want me and there's no way I'm going to live with somebody who doesn't want me. I'd rather stick pins in my eyes."

Mr. Grice looked at her in consternation. It had been a trying morning and he had a feeling that it was about to get worse. What was the matter with his supervisor that she was always giving him the difficult jobs?

"But Mrs. Thomas is your legal guardian," he tried.

"I'm not going," Martine repeated stubbornly, "and you can't make me."

Mr. Grice gathered his papers together in a messy bundle, knocking over a glass of water in the process. "I'll be back," he told Martine, ignoring the puddle and the ink turning to watercolor on his documents. "I have to make a phone call."

Martine sat staring at the smoke-stained wallpaper in Mr. Grices's office feeling much more afraid than she'd let on. The past few weeks had been a blur. For the first nightmarish five days after the fire she'd stayed with the Morrisons, until their sons returned from a college rugby tour. Then she'd moved in with a friend of her mother's who was unable to cope with a grieving child. Finally, she was driven off to the house of Miss Rose, her English teacher, who was going to take care of her until her future was decided. Everywhere she went, people wore over-bright smiles and were full of helpful suggestions. But as soon as she left the room, she could hear hushed conversations in which the words *orphan* and *all alone in the world* were frequently used.

Martine was too dazed and heartbroken to care. Most of the time she walked around with a crashing sensation in her head, as if she were falling into a well with no bottom. She couldn't eat, she couldn't sleep, she couldn't cry. The question she kept asking herself over and over was *why?* Why had she been saved and her parents hadn't? It seemed so unfair. The firemen had praised her bravery and told her she'd done the right thing. They said if she'd opened her door even a crack to try to get to her parents, she would have been swallowed by the blaze. But it was hard not to feel guilty. And what happened to her now? Was she really going to be sent away to a stranger in South Africa?

It was then that she spotted a cream envelope on Mr. Grice's desk. There was something familiar about it. She picked it up and studied the return address. It was written in neat blue pen: Gwyn Thomas, Sawubona Game Reserve, Cape Province, South Africa. Martine searched her memory. Where had she seen that handwriting before? Then it came back to her. She'd watched her mum opening these envelopes every month for as long as she could remember. Nothing had ever been said about them, but Martine had always detected a change in her mum after she'd read the letters. She seemed to smile more, to laugh more easily. To Martine, sitting abandoned and confused among Mr. Grice's dusty files, it was all the more upsetting that her mum had never told her that the letters came from her grandmother, or even that she had a grandmother at all. Why was it such a secret?

Martine thought about the signature on the letter: Gwyn Thomas. It sounded so stern. She found it difficult to grasp that such a person might be her grandmother, let alone that she might have to call her Grandmother or, worse still, Granny. She couldn't even think of her as Gwyn. For some reason the whole name—Gwyn Thomas—stuck in her head.

Mr. Grice returned to the office shaking his head. "I'm afraid your options are extremely limited," he said. "I've managed to find you a bed in the orphanage in Upper Blickley—"

"It's okay," Martine interrupted, "I've decided I'll go to South Africa after all."

Mr. Grice heaved a huge sigh of relief. "Well," he said, "that settles it."

Right from the start, it was obvious that everyone around Martine was much more excited about her new future than she was. "A *game reserve* in *Africa*," said Miss Rose in awe. "Just think, Martine, it'll be like spending your life on safari."

Mrs. Morrison seemed to be convinced she'd be eaten by a tiger. "You'll have to be vigilant," she told Martine. "But oh, what an adventure it'll all be!"

Martine rolled her eyes. Mrs. Morrison was the kindest woman in the world, but she was absolutely clueless when it came to the animal kingdom. "There are no tigers in

Africa," Martine had to keep telling her. "Not unless they're in zoos."

Apart from that one detail, she herself knew very little about Africa. When she tried to picture it, all she could come up with was big yellow plains, umbrella trees, mangoes, dark faces, and baking hot sun. She wondered if wild animals literally roamed the streets. Would she be able to have one as a pet? Martine's mum had been allergic to animals, so Martine had always been kept away from them, but ever since she was tiny she'd yearned to have one of her own. Perhaps she could get a monkey.

Then she remembered the tone of her grandmother's letter and the crashing feeling came surging back. Gwyn Thomas didn't sound like the kind of person who would say yes to a primate in her living room. If she even *had* a living room. For all Martine knew, her grandmother could live in a grass hut.

At school, most of her classmates seemed to have forgotten that barely three weeks had gone by since her home had burned to the ground and that she was hardly going to South Africa out of choice. "You're *sooo* lucky," they kept telling her. "You'll be able to learn to surf and everything. It'll be so cool."

Listening to them, Martine thought that the one good thing about moving to Africa was that she'd never again have to enter the grim gates of Bodley Brook School. She didn't fit in here. Come to think of it, she'd never fit in anywhere with children her own age, but somehow it hadn't mattered when her mum and dad were around, because *they* were her best friends. Her dad had been a doctor who worked very long hours, but in the summer he took time off and they'd go camping in Cornwall, where her mum would paint and she and her dad would swim or fish or he'd teach her a little first aid. And every weekend, come rain or shine, they always had fun, even if it was only making pancakes. Now it was over and there was a hole in Martine's heart.

On Saturday morning, the day before she was due to fly to Cape Town, Miss Rose took her shopping for summer clothes on Oxford Street in London. An icy gray rain was falling and the entire road was a sea of frenzied shoppers and tourists poking umbrellas in each other's eyes, but nothing could dampen Miss Rose's enthusiasm.

"Look at these cute shorts!" she said to Martine as they fought their way around the Gap. "What a great baseball cap! Oh, I can just see you in this stripy red T-shirt."

Martine just let her go on. If the truth be known, she felt ill. Her stomach was a bubbling cauldron of nerves and her mouth was dry with fear at the prospect of what tomorrow would bring. "Whatever you think," she kept saying as Miss Rose presented her with clothing options. "Yes, it's nice. Yes, I'm sure it'll be fine."

She ended up with two pairs of khaki shorts, a pair of jeans, four T-shirts, a baseball cap, and a pair of tough, camel-colored hiking boots. The only time she was forced to put up a fight was when Miss Rose tried to insist on a floral-print dress. Martine, who had cropped brown hair and bright green eyes, had refused to wear a dress since the age of five, and she had no intention of starting now.

"I'll get bitten by a snake if I don't have proper protection," she told Miss Rose.

"But surely you run the same risk if you wear shorts," protested her teacher.

"Yes," said Martine, "but that's *different*. Have you ever seen an explorer who didn't wear shorts?"

Back in Hampshire that evening, Miss Rose cooked a farewell dinner for Martine—a roast chicken with crispy potatoes, garden peas, homemade Yorkshire pudding, and onion gravy. Mr. and Mrs. Morrison came over and Mrs. Morrison presented Martine with a pair of binoculars that had belonged to an old uncle.

"To help you spot the big cats," she told Martine.

Martine was very moved, particularly when Mrs. Morrison also gave her a large slice of homemade chocolate cake carefully packed in a lunch box for her journey.

"I wish you much happiness, dear," Mrs. Morrison said emotionally. "Remember that you'll always have a home with Mr. Morrison and me."

Mr. Morrison just grunted in agreement. He was a man of few words. But when his wife turned away to thank the teacher for the meal, he put his hand in his coat pocket and brought out a carved wooden box. "To keep you safe," he said in a low voice, giving it to Martine. Then he opened his car door and started the engine.

"Ready, love," he called to Mrs. Morrison. "See you, then, Martine."

Martine waited until she was alone in Miss Rose's spare room that night to open the box. Inside she found a pink Maglite flashlight, a Swiss Army knife, and a first-aid kit. She could hardly believe her eyes. She laid everything out on the bed and spent several rapturous minutes reading the survival leaflet that accompanied it all. The generosity of everyone was very touching. After a while, she repacked her presents carefully, turned off the light, and lay on the bed. A full moon beamed in through the window, laying a silver path across the room.

Despite herself, Martine began to feel excited. By tomorrow night she'd be on a plane bound for Africa and a life she could not even begin to imagine. For better or worse, Fate was closing a door on the past.

3

The first thing Martine noticed was the heat. It rose from the airport runway in a soupy, silvery haze so thick that the horizon appeared to bow under the weight of the blue sky, and all the planes had wavy edges as if in a dream. Back in England, it had been a freezing winter's night, with the weather report forecasting gales and heavy snow, but here Martine felt as if she were burning up. She stood without moving, a small, deathly pale eleven-year-old, and watched the other passengers board the yellow bus to the terminal.

"Wake up, love, you don't want to be left behind." A bald man in a Billabong surf shirt was leaning over her. "Where's Mum and Dad? Are they waiting for you?"

Martine wanted to burst into tears and scream so loudly that everyone in the airport could hear her: "Yes, actually, I do want to be left behind. And no, my mum and dad are not waiting. They'll never be waiting."

Instead she mumbled: "I—I'm just . . . I'm not . . . I . . . Somebody's meeting me."

"You don't sound very sure."

"Harry, what are you *doing*? I'm fed up to the back teeth with you. The bus is leaving and if you're not here in five seconds, so am I," a woman called shrilly.

"I'll be fine," Martine told the man. "Thanks for asking."

"Really?" He reached out a damp pink paw and patted her hard on the shoulder. "Cheer up, love. You're in Africa now."

The woman at the information desk at Cape Town airport tapped a little drum roll on the counter with her purple nails and squinted over Martine's head at the line that was beginning to form. Her name tag described her as *Noeleen Henshaw, Assistant Supervisor.*

"My girl, it's not that I don't want to help you," she told Martine in a nasal voice, "but I'm going to need a few more details. Now, what does your grandmother look like?"

Martine tried to conjure up a picture of the grandmother she had never seen. "Well, I . . ."

"Do you have a phone number for your grandmother?"

"Just an address," admitted Martine. For much of her journey, she'd been taken care of by a cheery flight attendant named Hayley whose job it was to "look after unaccompanied minors," but as soon as they landed in South Africa, Hayley had pointed her in the direction of the airport bus and just as cheerily waved good-bye.

Noeleen gave an exasperated shake of her henna-red hair and looked again at the line. "Sweetie, I think the best thing for you to do is to sit over there, where I can keep an eye on you. If your grandmother doesn't show up, I'll try to find someone to help you."

"Okay," Martine said uncertainly. "Thank you."

She picked up her suitcase and her new olive-green backpack—a present from Miss Rose—and walked into the arrivals hall, taking a seat under the *Welcome to South Africa* sign. Never in her life had she felt less welcome. More than an hour had gone by since her plane had landed in Cape Town and still no one had arrived to collect her. Martine was close to tears. Her worst fears had been realized. Her grandmother hadn't wanted her and so she hadn't bothered to come and fetch her. What Martine was going to do now with no money and nowhere to stay, she had absolutely no idea.

Added to which, she was weak with hunger. It was ten o'clock in the morning and all she'd had to eat since the previous evening was Mrs. Morrison's chocolate cake. The food on the plane had been inedible. The scrambled eggs were watery, the rolls had the consistency of tennis balls, and the main meal smelled like pet food. Martine made up

19

her mind that she would never fly again without extensive supplies of cake and maybe some ham sandwiches for good measure. Opposite her, a smiling customer left the Juicy Lucy stand with a smoothie and a large muffin. Martine's stomach rumbled enviously.

"Miss Martine, you will be thinking we have forgotten you," boomed a voice so deep that it rumbled in her chest like a bass drum. Martine looked up to see a mahogany giant bearing down on her, arms outstretched and the broadest smile in Africa on his face. He had a scar in the shape of a question mark on one shining cheek and a tooth on a leather thong around his neck. He was wearing a bush hat with a zebra-skin band, and khaki hunter-type clothing that had seen better days.

"Miss Martine?" he queried. Without waiting for her to reply, he gripped her hand and pumped it up and down furiously. "I'm Tendai," he said. "I'm very, very happy to meet you. Your grandmother has told me all about you. She was very sorry that she couldn't be here to collect you, but, oh, what a morning we have had! Late last night we received a call to say that, due to a mix-up with some paperwork, a shipment of elephants we were expecting next weekend was being delivered early this morning. There was nobody to supervise their arrival except your grandmother and myself, and she had to stay until the vet had checked each one. I offered to fetch you instead. I forgot that a man of the bush knows nothing about the highway! I have been driving all over Cape Town! I hope you can forgive me. I will get you home to Sawubona just as fast as I can."

Martine hardly knew how to respond to this torrent of words, but she immediately warmed to the big, gentle man who delivered them. He carried nature with him, almost like an aura.

"Pleased to meet you, Tendai," she said, adding shyly, "Of course I forgive you."

At these words, Tendai laughed. Picking up her suitcase and tucking it under one arm as if it weighed no more than a hen, he led the way out into the sunshine.

4

Afterward Martine would always remember her first journey to Sawubona, a name that Tendai explained was a Zulu greeting. He was from the Zulu tribe himself. They took the coastal road out of Cape Town, riding in his battered jeep past a series of magical bays and inlets where the sea was navy blue against the clear sky. Some beaches were wild, with flying spray and forests growing almost to the shore. Some had rainbow beach huts and surfers riding the breakers on bright boards. Some had rocky colonies of penguins or seals. And all of them were overlooked by the mauve-gray cliffs of a flat-topped mountain, which was called, for obvious reasons, Table Mountain.

After about an hour they turned inland and Martine

was amazed at how quickly the scenery changed from a heathery type of vegetation and became like the Africa she'd always seen in photographs. Pale spiky thorn trees and ragged shrubs dotted the long yellow grass, which glowed beneath the blazing summer sun as if it was lit from underneath. The empty road stretched on forever. Martine rolled down her window in the hot cab and the dusty, animal smell of the bush poured into the jeep.

Tendai talked about Sawubona along the way, describing his job as a tracker at the game reserve. Sawubona, it turned out, was not just a game reserve, it was a wildlife sanctuary, and it was Tendai's role to check on the progress of every animal in the park. About a quarter of the animals at Sawubona had been born there, but all the rest had been rescued. Some came from drought-stricken areas or game reserves or zoos that had gone out of business. Others had been brought to Sawubona with injuries or because they'd been orphaned in hunts or culls.

"In twenty years," Tendai said, "I never saw Henry Thomas, your grandfather, turn a single animal away. Not even one."

This was the first mention there had been of her grandfather, and Martine pricked up her ears. But Tendai's next sentence caught her totally off guard.

"I'm so sorry, Miss Martine, that I wasn't there at his side, watching over him, the night that he died."

Martine's head was already spinning from jet lag and lack of food, and this news made it spin a little more. It was clear that it hadn't occurred to Tendai that she might not know she even had a grandfather, let alone that he had died.

She said carefully, "Would it be okay if you told me what happened?"

Tendai's hands tightened on the steering wheel. "Yebo," he said. "I can try."

It turned out that nearly two years had passed since her grandfather's death and yet the events surrounding it were still shrouded in mystery. The police theory was that Henry had stumbled upon a gang of poachers trying to steal a couple of giraffes or maybe kill them for trophies. It had happened on a weekend when Tendai was away in the north of the country visiting his relatives—a weekend when Sawubona was at its most vulnerable. There had been a struggle. When it was over, Henry had been fatally wounded and the giraffes left for dead.

"There was no telephone in the village where I was staying," said Tendai, "so I never knew that this terrible thing had happened until I returned on Monday. By then it was much too late. In the summer, many Zulus ask the Rain Queen to bless their fields with rain, but that week it seems she had been listening far too well. For two days, the storms had been washing away the tracks, and the police and their vehicles had been driving all over the grounds. By the third day, when I came, there was no sign to be found."

None of the hunters had ever been caught. To this day, nobody knew whether Henry had been murdered or just shot by accident in the struggle. Most puzzling of all was why the poachers had fled without the giraffes they had so obviously come for.

"Did the police manage to find any clues?" Martine asked worriedly. It was sad to hear about her grandfather, but it was even more disturbing to know there were killers on the loose in the very place she was expected to make her new home.

"Tch, those baboons! Don't worry, little one, even the spider leaves a trail. It might take some years, but eventually we will find those who did this. Maybe, if we are patient enough, they will even find us."

The Zulu's face had darkened during the conversation and now he gave himself a little shake, as though remembering that he and Martine had only just met and perhaps he was saying more than he should. He smiled his amazing smile. "Your grandfather had a warrior's heart," he told her. "He was the *best* game warden. Number one."

Martine felt a pang for the grandfather she had never known. He sounded like a good man. The new game warden was a young man by the name of Alex du Preez. There was something in the way that Tendai said his name that gave Martine the impression that Mr. du Preez was not on Tendai's list of top-ten favorite people.

They were passing a village of thatched huts and scattered houses with sunflowers and maize stalks in the yards. A group of African children were playing soccer in a field.

The jeep slowed and turned onto a driveway overhung by banana palms. At the end of it was a pale green house with a corrugated iron roof. A peeling Coca-Cola sign was propped against one wall. Three chickens wandered out through the front door.

Martine climbed out of the jeep. "Is this my grand-mother's house?" she asked, unable to hide her surprise. She wasn't sure what she was expecting, but it wasn't this.

"No, chile, Tendai is jus' bringin' you to see me."

Martine turned around to see one of the fattest women she had ever encountered waddling toward her across the threadbare lawn. She was wearing a traditional African dress in the most brilliant colors, with a matching head-scarf of banana yellow, Kalahari red, and lime green. "I tole him you would be hungry," the woman continued in a voice as warm as buttermilk, "and I see I'm right. Look at you, chile, you just skin 'n' bone."

"Miss Martine, meet my aunt, Miss Grace," said Tendai with evident pride. "The best cook in the world."

They followed Grace into the little green house. The smells coming from the kitchen were divine.

She and Tendai made themselves comfortable on hand-made wooden chairs in Grace's simple but spotless living room. There was a woven grass mat on the floor and an out-of-date calendar on the wall, depicting a tropical island.

In a matter of minutes Grace emerged from the kitchen with two huge plates containing omelettes made from fresh farm eggs and wild mushrooms, a heap of crispy bacon, and tomatoes fried with brown sugar. Martine felt as if she hadn't eaten in years and she savored every mouthful in silence. By the time she had finished, she agreed with Tendai wholeheartedly: Grace *was* the best cook in the world.

She turned to Grace to thank her and found the woman watching her intently.

"Chile looks just like Veronica," Grace commented to Tendai.

Martine jumped as if she had been scalded. "You knew my mum?" she cried.

"Aunt!" shouted Tendai, leaping to his feet. "I told you not to say anything."

"Quiet, boy," ordered Grace. "There be too many secrets at Sawubona. The chile has a right to know the truth."

"What truth?" demanded Martine.

"Miss Martine," said Tendai, "I'm sorry, we must go now."

"But . . ."

"Please!"

Martine looked from one to the other, her head buzzing with questions that it was clear she was not going to be allowed to ask. Grudgingly, she followed Tendai out to the jeep. Grace grabbed her arm. "Wait," she said. She put her hand on Martine's forehead and Martine felt an electric current pass through her. Grace's eyes widened.

"You have the gift, chile," she whispered. "Jus' like the forefathers said."

"What gift?" Martine whispered back.

But Grace just shook her head. "Be very careful. The gift can be a blessin' or a curse. Make your decisions wisely."

5

In the yard, Tendai had the engine running. As soon as Martine climbed into the jeep, he put his foot on the accelerator and they bounded over the potholed drive and onto the main road. Heat wavered like a watery mirage above the pavement.

Tendai seemed agitated. "I'm sorry, Miss Martine. I shouldn't have taken you there. Perhaps you would be kind enough not to mention it to your grandmother."

Martine barely heard him. Her forehead was still tingling from the pressure of Grace's hand, and her mind was rushing like an express train through her past. She was trying to remember something, *anything*, that would explain what had just happened.

"But what did Grace mean about my mum? Did *she* ever live at Sawubona?"

"Please," begged Tendai. "Those things you must ask your grandmother."

He drove on in silence for a few minutes, before turning right onto a sandy road lined with a high wire fence. Arching over the entrance and supported by two white pillars was a black wooden sign etched with the words *Sawubona Game Reserve*.

The jeep stopped and Tendai pointed out of the window. "Can you see the buffalo?"

Martine dragged herself reluctantly back to the present. She squinted into the sun, but could see nothing except an endless expanse of trees, dusty shrubs, and grass, sprawling under an electric-blue sky. On the horizon was a range of mauve mountains. A black eagle circled lazily overhead.

"No," she sighed. "I can't."

"Don't look *through* the bush," instructed Tendai, "look *into* the bush."

Martine did and gradually the shrubs resolved themselves into the muscular black hides of around thirty buffalo. She could make out their curved horns and intense faces between the trees.

Then she spotted the bull elephant. He was standing under an umbrella tree, his curved tusks and gray bulk almost completely camouflaged. Like the buffalo, he seemed as ancient as the land itself. But even from three hundred yards away, his deadly power was apparent.

Martine stared at him in awe. She was beginning to feel overwhelmed by all she had seen and heard since leaving the airport. "Wow!" she said at last. "He's huge and so . . . so still. I've only ever seen wild animals on television. What else do you have here?"

"Twelve other elephants," Tendai recited proudly, "eight ostriches, one hundred and fifty springboks, ten wildebeest, eighteen kudus, twenty zebras, six lions, four leopards, seven warthogs, a couple of troops of baboons, a few waterbucks, and a . . ." He stopped. "That's all."

"And what? You were going to say something else."

"It's nothing," Tendai said. "The local tribes believe that a white giraffe has come to Sawubona. The Africans have a legend, which says that the child who can ride a white giraffe will have power over all the animals, but it is only a myth. We have had no giraffes, not even ordinary giraffes, at Sawubona for nearly two years now, but people keep coming to me to report that they've seen this white one. The tribesmen say that it's an albino giraffe, as white as a snow leopard. If it's true, that would make it one of the rarest animals in the world. There is no proof. I have never seen it, and I am in the game reserve every day."

Martine had an odd feeling of déjà vu, almost as if she'd had this conversation in another life. "But do *you* believe it exists?" she asked eagerly.

Tendai shrugged. "From time to time, I have seen tracks, but they always disappear. I follow them for a few hundred yards and then they just vanish into thin air."

"So maybe it *is* true!"

The Zulu laughed. "It is not always the one you follow who makes the tracks, little one. In the old times, some tribes would tie the hooves of animals to their feet to lead other hunters away from the herds, and your grandmother says that in the mountains of Asia people have tried to fake the footprints of the Abominable Snowman. Maybe this is what is happening here!" He grinned at Martine. "If the white giraffe does exist," he said, "it must be very shy."

The gears clanked and they moved off down the road. When they reached a high iron gate, Tendai jumped out to open it. On the other side was a driveway lined with huge red and orange flowers, an immaculate lawn, and a white-painted thatched house. Nerves bit into Martine's stomach. In a few minutes, she would meet her grandmother for the first time. Would Gwyn Thomas be glad to see her? Would she be kind? Would she, even though she hadn't really wanted her, learn to like Martine? And what if she didn't? What then?

6

The door of the thatched house opened and out stepped a tall, slender woman in her early sixties, wearing jeans and a short-sleeved khaki shirt with a symbol of a lion on the pocket. Her hair was tied back in a ponytail. Martine was still taking in the fact that her grandmother was dressed in denim when Gwyn Thomas marched up to her and, without any introduction, took her face in both hands. Up close, Martine could see that her fair hair was streaked with white and that her chestnut-brown skin was etched with a million creases. She looked at Martine with an expression that was impossible to read.

"You're all grown up," was all she said. She turned to

Tendai. "You're very late, my friend. You haven't been visiting that crazy old magic woman, have you?"

Martine realized with a shock that she was referring to Grace. "We got lost, Grandmother," she said quickly. "We were driving all over Cape Town. I've seen the whole city!"

In a flash, her grandmother turned on her. "In this house, we speak only when we are spoken to." She wheeled around abruptly and stalked back inside.

Tendai followed her with Martine's suitcase. He didn't look at Martine as he passed.

Martine walked after them, her heart thumping. A ginger cat sat washing itself on the front step. It regarded her curiously as she approached.

"Oh, boy, this is going to be fun," Martine muttered under her breath. But the ginger cat simply yawned, closed its eyes, and lay down in the sun to sleep.

Tendai appeared at the door. "Your grandmother is waiting for you," he said.

With Tendai gone, Martine felt more alone than ever. She stepped into the house and looked around. It was cool and peaceful inside, with polished stone floors and big, comfy, worn leather chairs. Another cat, this one black and white, was curled up on the lid of an old piano and there were oil paintings of cheetahs and elephants on the walls. The bare beams and thatch gave the room a sense of space and calmness.

Her grandmother emerged from the kitchen with a glass of milk and a plate of egg sandwiches. She motioned for

Martine to take a seat at the dining table. Martine hated egg sandwiches and she was still full of Grace's delicious food, but she wasn't about to say so. She began picking at the bread.

"I don't have fizzy drinks here," her grandmother said. "Don't believe in them." She stood at the head of the table like a lioness, her blue eyes locked on Martine as if in challenge.

"Okay," Martine said warily.

"The first things you need to know are the rules of my house. Please don't touch anything that doesn't belong to you, and that includes the piano. No running, no shouting, no cursing, no sweets. I don't have a television. I go into Cape Town twice a year, so there'll be no shopping for you. No fast food. We grow our own vegetables. You'll be expected to make your own bed and help out around here. I can't abide laziness. Any questions?"

"Can I breathe?" Martine asked cheekily.

"No answering back!" her grandmother roared.

Martine shrank into her chair. The egg sandwiches lay untouched.

"Give them to me," her grandmother said, snatching them up. "I should have known that crazy old woman would be cooking for you. Well, you can eat them for dinner. I won't tolerate waste."

The rest of the day went downhill from there. Martine was dizzy and a bit tearful after the long flight and the adventures of the morning, but after she'd showered, her grandmother insisted on driving her to the tiny town nearby—a single street of shops known as Storm Crossing—to buy a school uniform and some brown lace-up shoes. At the clothing store, where she was fitted with two white shirts, two navy blue skirts, a Windbreaker, a blazer that had a lynx cat with fur-tipped ears on the badge, and a gray tie, Martine discovered to her horror that she was expected to start school the very next day, without even the shortest break to adjust to her new surroundings.

"There'll be plenty of time for that," her grandmother told her. "You've missed too much school already."

As if that wasn't bad enough, at dinner (thankfully, not the egg sandwiches, which weren't mentioned) Martine slipped on the polished floor as she carried her grandmother's favorite teapot back to the kitchen. It smashed to pieces.

"Oh, what *was* Veronica thinking?" her grandmother ranted. "I knew this would happen. How can I be expected to look after a child?"

She refused to allow Martine to help clean up the mess. Martine just crept quietly upstairs to bed with tears running down her face. She felt utterly bereft. She was in deepest, darkest Africa with no parents and no friends, living with a grandmother who plainly couldn't stand the sight of her. Really, it couldn't get any worse.

As far as Martine could tell, there was only one positive in her new life, and that was Sawubona itself. She was already falling in love with it. The sun had been setting over the game reserve when they returned from the shops, and a herd of springboks was moving in a dusty column down to the water hole in front of the house. Martine had managed to escape from her grandmother's clutches long enough to go down to the bottom of the garden and watch the springboks through the high game fence.

She'd had to pinch herself several times. Yesterday she'd woken up shivering in gray, gloomy England and now, just a day later, she was sitting under a copper sky streaked with purple, with the evening sun warm on her skin. The young springboks were bouncing around the shallows as if they had mini-trampolines attached to their hooves, and the guinea fowl, which she'd earlier seen waddling along the roadside like plump, blue-speckled kings, were crying in the trees as they settled down to roost. Martine stretched out on the grass and let her nose fill with the heady smells of an African evening—cooking fires, wild animals, herby grass, and nature in abundance. She'd never experienced anything quite like it.

Her bedroom, too, was something a bit special. It was up in the attic, with a window cut into the thatch. Although very tiny, it had plenty of character and charm. There was a bookcase crammed with books about animals and Africa against one wall and a bed made with crisp white sheets, a patchwork quilt, and large soft pillows. But the best part was that it overlooked the water hole, a brown dam surrounded by thorny bush. Tendai had told her that most of the reserve's wildlife gathered there at dawn or at sunset.

Now, however, it was nighttime. The mattress sank beneath Martine's weight. She dried her eyes on her sleeve and wondered if it was really true that her mum had lived at Sawubona. It cheered her to imagine that this might once have been Veronica's room; Veronica might have read these books or snuggled into this very quilt. But why on earth had she never told Martine about this place?

So tired that she could barely put on her pajamas, Martine slid between the sheets, her head whirling with snapshots from the long day. The last thing she thought about before she went to sleep was the white giraffe.

7

The next morning Martine woke feeling as if she were going to the dentist. For a long time she lay there with her eyes screwed tightly shut, because that way she could pretend that none of it had happened. Her home had not burned down, and her mum and dad were not gone forever, and she had not been sent to the wilds of Africa to live with a total stranger. Finally, when she could avoid it no longer, she opened her eyes. A vast sky of the most incredible blue filled her vision. The clock on the bedside table said 6:05 A.M. Right on cue, an orange-breasted bird fluttered onto a thatch beam outside her window and began singing a song of pure happiness. *Tirrootiree, tirrootiree.*

Propping herself up on one elbow, Martine gazed out over the game reserve. The water hole was draped with early-morning mist and streaked with gold from the sun. A dozen or so elephants were splashing around in it, wallowing in the mud and spraying each other with their trunks. Zebras were grazing nearby. She shook her head in wonder. The scene didn't take away the anguish in her heart, but it definitely helped.

Even so, she walked downstairs on leaden feet. Her grandmother was sitting at the kitchen table, her hands wrapped around a coffee mug. When Martine entered, she stood up quickly and said, "Good morning, Martine, I hope you slept well." Her voice shook slightly, as though she was nervous. Before Martine could speak, she went on hurriedly, "There are boiled eggs in the pan and some bread in the toaster and anything else you might need on the kitchen table. On the counter over there, you'll find a lunch box containing sunscreen, yellow cling peaches from the garden, and some cheese and chutney sandwiches. I have to go out now to feed the young elephant, but I'll be back at seven thirty to take you to school."

Martine was still stammering a thank you when the door banged behind her grandmother and a gust of cool air blew in. It wasn't an apology, but Martine already knew that it was all she was going to get.

The dentist feeling returned on the fifteen-minute drive to school, most of which Martine spent squirming in her new uniform, hating the skirt and not knowing what to say to her grandmother. And it didn't diminish when Gwyn Thomas drove her through the gates of Caracal School and she saw the hordes of healthy, confident children who were to be her new schoolmates. They were every shade of honey, cappuccino, and chocolate. None were the color of Martine—that is to say, a sort of unhealthy gray white. After her grandmother had left her at the door of the headmistress's office with a gruff but kindly "Have a good day. Tendai or I will collect you at four," she stood pressed against the wall, trying to be as inconspicuous as possible.

"Be with you in a mo," called a voice when she knocked. Martine could hear someone speaking on the phone. While she waited, she took in her surroundings. Her old school, Bodley Brook, had resembled a concrete prison, with a blacktop playground and peeling beige corridors reeking of disinfectant. The bathrooms had been covered in graffiti. This place didn't even look like a school. It was more like a lovely campsite. Log buildings made from glowing chestnut timber were scattered about grounds laid with emerald lawns and huge trees. Behind a wooden fence, a swimming pool sparkled.

"You can close your mouth now. We still have the same boring old lessons you had back home. You know, long division, dead kings, punctuation!"

The expression on Martine's face must have said it all,

because the Cleopatra-haired vision standing in the doorway wearing wooden parrot earrings and a long purple dress laughed merrily and, pulling her into the room, added, "Only joking. Our lessons are, of course, extremely interesting. I'm Elaine Rathmore, the headmistress, and you must be Martine. Welcome to Caracal."

Once she'd gotten used to Mrs. Rathmore's sense of humor, Martine couldn't help liking the headmistress, who was very down-to-earth. Mrs. Rathmore explained that despite appearances, Caracal was a school like any other, but it did have a strong focus on the environment. All the buildings were heated with solar energy, many school projects concerned conservation, and the cafeteria served only organic meals. They went through a copy of the rules together and Mrs. Rathmore explained the schedule. Then they went for a tour of the grounds. Apparently sports were a "big deal" at Caracal School, which had produced many champions. There was a gym with a climbing wall, and the sports fields stretched for several acres.

"If you have a gift for sports—or anything else, for that matter—we'll find it," Mrs. Rathmore promised.

Martine, who knew perfectly well that she didn't have a gift for sports—had in fact been hopeless at every sport she ever tried—thought back to Grace's words: *You have the gift, just like the forefathers said.* What *was* the gift? Was it to do with science, math, art, or even music? Or something she couldn't even guess at? *Be careful*, Grace had cautioned her. *The gift can be a blessing or a curse. Make your decisions wisely.*

41

What kind of gift came with a warning?

"Lucy van Heerden . . . one of our talented prefects," Mrs. Rathmore was saying. "Lucy is in Miss Volkner's class with you, Martine. Martine? We haven't sent you to sleep already, have we?"

Martine blinked.

An elegant blond girl was standing in front of her holding out her hand. Martine shook it and was surprised to find that it was ice cold. Judging by Lucy's caramel tan, she spent every spare hour surfing or sunning herself on the beach.

After asking Lucy to take Martine under her wing, show her the ropes, and give her a "very special Caracal School welcome," Mrs. Rathmore went on her way in a billowing cloud of purple, leaving Martine with her glamorous new classmate.

"Jeesh, but you're white," Lucy commented as soon as the headmistress was out of earshot. "Where are you from? Iceland?"

"England," mumbled Martine. If she was awkward and self-conscious to begin with, she now felt a million times worse.

Lucy giggled. "I'm kidding," she said, giving Martine a friendly punch that almost knocked her over. "Come on, we're late for Miss Volkner's class, but at break I'll introduce you to the rest of the gang."

At lunchtime Martine discovered that the gang to which Lucy had referred was the Five Star Gang, a group of the most popular kids in the school. Along with Lucy, there was her twin brother, Luke, also blond and good-looking with caramel skin; Scott Henderson, who was driven to school each morning in a red Lamborghini; the school rugby captain, Pieter Booker; and a black boy named Xhosa (which, if you were English and couldn't make the clicking noise that the Africans made, was pronounced "Corza") Washington, who was the son of the local mayor. They all had the latest haircuts and a way of wearing their uniforms that made them seem like designer clothes. Most kids idolized them and over the coming weeks Martine noticed that even the teachers seemed to give them special treatment.

During break, Lucy introduced Martine to the Five Star boys and several other children. On the whole, they seemed a friendly bunch, and a couple of them went out of their way to make her feel included. Martine sat in the sunshine eating her cheese and chutney sandwiches, smiling and nodding, and wondering how it was possible to be in such a pretty place, surrounded by laughing children, and still feel like the loneliest, most miserable girl on earth. All the old feelings that she'd had at Bodley Brook came flooding back. It was not just that she felt shy and clumsy. She didn't fit in at all. None of the things they talked about—surfing, hair gel, music—interested her. But what did interest her? Martine didn't know. Reading, she supposed. And the white giraffe. She was very, very interested in the white giraffe.

It was while she was thinking about this that she noticed

a small figure sitting alone under a tree in the distance.

"Oh, *him,*" Lucy said with distaste when Martine asked what the child was doing there. Her nose wrinkled. "He's either deaf, stupid, or a nutcase. We can't work out which."

Over the next few days, Martine learned that the boy's name was Ben and that he was of mixed race, with a Zulu father and an Indian mother—a dancer from Rajasthan, so the story went. Martine was small for her age, but he was as thin as she was and not much taller. If you looked at Ben closely, you could see that he was far from weak. His brown arms and legs were strong and wiry. But most children didn't take enough interest in Ben to find that out. He was an outcast. Hardly anyone ever spoke to him. This was partly because in the three years he'd been at the school, Ben had never uttered a syllable. The teachers had long since accepted that he was mute, mainly because he answered their questions on bits of paper and was consistently top of the class, but to the Five Star Gang, who claimed they'd once seen him holding a completely normal conversation with his dad in the parking lot, he was a source of both irritation and amusement. Every lunchtime, he would take his backpack and disappear to the farthest corner of the school playing fields. There, he would sit under a tree and read a book. His nickname was Buddha Ben, because he had a habit of burning incense and never retaliated if you stole his book or forced him to do your homework.

Martine found it upsetting that everyone was so mean

to him. She made up her mind to try to befriend him, but the first afternoon an opportunity presented itself Lucy waved her over and asked her what she was up to and she couldn't bring herself to admit that she'd been on her way to talk to "Bonkers Ben," as Lucy called him. The next day she put it off for some other reason, and after a while she stopped thinking about Ben altogether.

8

Those early days at Sawubona were among the hardest of Martine's life. At times, she felt as if she were undergoing some sort of test, almost as if she were being prepared for something. Everything added to her sense of isolation. It was like being a castaway on a desert island. There was no one she could turn to for comfort or advice. No one who would hold her if she cried. Certainly not her grandmother. Still, she couldn't help noticing that whenever she was feeling particularly upset or down, Gwyn Thomas would suddenly and unexpectedly make an apricot pie for dinner and serve it up with whipped cream, or leave a vase of wildflowers on her bedside table, or say something like, "Martine,

I could do with your help when I go to feed the baby elephant tonight."

The little elephant lived in an enclosure in the sanctuary close to Tendai's house. He had been rescued from a Zambian zoo that had gone out of business. Tendai had named him Shaka, after the legendary Zulu warrior king.

"So he'll grow up to be a great leader for the herd, despite his early trials, just like Shaka," was his remark to Martine.

Shaka was one of several animals in the sanctuary, which was a sort of hospital and holding area for new arrivals before they were relocated to the main game reserve. At present, Tendai and Samson, a wizened, white-haired man who looked at least 104 years old, were tending to a jackal that had been hit by a car and had a leg in a cast, an owl with an infected eye, a springbok with a nasty abscess, and an orphaned bush baby. The bush baby was one of the sweetest creatures Martine had ever seen, with huge brown eyes in a tiny gray apelike face, a long curling tail, and paws like a koala, made for climbing.

One of Martine's chores was to make sure the sanctuary animals had water morning and evening, and she'd also been allowed to feed Shaka three times. Once, when she was giggling at his wobbly gait and funny pink mouth gulping at his milk pail, she'd caught her grandmother watching her with an enigmatic, almost pleased expression. But even on those occasions when she seemed to be making an effort to be nice, Martine still couldn't shake the feeling that her grandmother didn't want her there.

Much to her frustration, she hadn't yet been allowed into the game reserve itself. Martine consoled herself with the thought that at least she could see the wildlife through the fence, and devoted all her spare time to reading up on the animals in the books she found in her room. She'd been fascinated by the facts she'd learned about giraffes. For instance, the spots on each giraffe are as unique as fingerprints; no two are alike. And although their necks are very long, they have the same number of vertebrae as other mammals—seven. Nowhere did she find any mention of white giraffes.

It was the animals at Sawubona that made Martine's life bearable. She'd never imagined she would live in a place with lions at the bottom of the garden. At night, when they were hunting, she could hear their spine-tingling roars, and just knowing she was so close to them was unbelievably thrilling. Curiously, creatures of all shapes and sizes seemed instinctively to know when she needed a friend. Take her grandmother's cats, Warrior and Shelby. They showed no interest in Martine at all except when she was feeling miserable, and then she could hardly move without them rubbing themselves against her legs and clamoring to sleep on her bed. And on two occasions the baboons had appeared in the garden when she'd had an awful day at school and performed so many funny antics that she got a cramp from laughing.

The second time it happened, Tendai came to the house on an errand while Martine was watching them. He crept up beside her and said teasingly, "So, little one, this is what you get up to when you are supposed to be doing your homework?"

Martine was spluttering an excuse when he cut her off with a chuckle. He told her that according to Zulu folklore, the baboons had once been lazy field hands. Instead of removing weeds from the crops, they spent their days sitting on their hoes, gossiping, or sleeping in the sunshine. They sat there for so long that eventually their hoes became tails and the weeds attached themselves to their bodies and became hair.

"You'd better watch out," Tendai said. "If you sit here too long without doing your homework, you might grow a tail and we'll have to put *you* in the game reserve." He grinned over her shoulder. "Isn't that right, Mrs. Thomas?"

Martine swung around guiltily to find her grandmother shaking with mirth, her blue eyes dancing.

"Tendai," Gwyn Thomas managed at last, "you're pure gold."

But none of this stopped Martine from lying awake at night aching for her mum and dad. Or from wondering about the secrets at Sawubona. After nearly three weeks on the game reserve, she was convinced that Grace was right—there *was* a wall of silence at Sawubona. Everything she asked about was met with the same blank response.

"A white giraffe!" exclaimed her grandmother when

Martine mentioned the tale Tendai had told her. "As if a white giraffe could go missing at Sawubona!"

"But Tendai said he saw some tracks."

"Martine, if there was a giraffe in the game reserve, don't you think that Tendai, who can track the path of a python across bare rock, would have found it by now?"

Martine had to admit her grandmother had a point.

But there were other secrets at Sawubona. For starters, there was the mystery of why her grandmother was on a mission to keep her out of the game reserve. And there was no question that that was what was going on. Sawubona was a private reserve, owned by her grandmother, but on weekdays it was open to tourists and visitors who prebooked appointments. They were guided around by the game warden, Alex du Preez, or Gwyn Thomas herself. That still left weekends. Yet every Saturday her grandmother had a thousand excuses for not allowing Martine to go into the reserve, from a shortage of staff to the late delivery of fuel to Sawubona. "You wouldn't want Tendai to run out of petrol when a charging elephant was around, would you, Martine?"

She'd also overheard Gwyn Thomas warning Tendai not to take Martine anywhere near Grace, to whom her grandmother again referred as that "crazy old magic woman."

"I won't have it," she told him. "I don't want her filling Martine's head with silly ideas. Grace is out of bounds as far as Martine is concerned."

All of this added to an air of secrecy that Martine could almost touch. She snooped about as much as she could and eavesdropped on one or two conversations, but she discovered nothing that could answer her biggest question: Why had Mum never told her about Sawubona? She'd found several books belonging to Veronica on her bookshelf and now knew her mum had probably spent much of her life here, but there was nothing to explain why she'd never told Martine about it.

Nor did Martine understand why her grandmother continued to maintain a stony silence on the subject. She found it odd that Gwyn Thomas never once said a word about her own daughter. Even if she was still grieving, one would have thought she might occasionally say something like: "This was your mum's favorite meal," or "Your mum loved to play the piano." But no, there was nothing. There were plenty of photographs of her grandfather, a silver-haired version of Harrison Ford, with her mum's sparkling green eyes, but none of her mum and dad, even though her grandmother had described them in her letter to Social Services as "the finest people I have ever known." And Tendai, who evidently did know something about her mum, refused point blank to give her any information.

"Please, Miss Martine," he kept saying, "you must ask your grandmother."

One evening, when Gwyn Thomas seemed to be in an unusually good mood, Martine plucked up the courage to do just that. A huge storm was raging outside and they had just eaten dinner.

"Grandmother," Martine began, "before Mr. Grice wrote to you, did you know about me?"

"Of course I did, Martine," said her grandmother impatiently. "What kind of question is that?"

"Then why didn't I know about you?"

"That's your mother's business and none of yours," her grandmother said, her voice rising. "Your mother made decisions in order to protect you. If you knew why she had done the things she did, you would be more grateful."

"How can I be grateful when no one will tell me the truth?" Martine burst out.

"Martine!" thundered her grandmother. "I won't tolerate this rudeness. Go to bed at once."

Martine jumped to her feet. "Fine," she said. "I will go to bed. But I am going to find out the truth about my mum and everything else that's going on around here, and nobody is going to stop me."

Upstairs, Martine sat on her bed watching rain lash the window. It was pitch black outside. Tears ran down her face. She'd lost count of the number of times she had cried since she had moved to Africa. She wished she could be back in England with Miss Rose or Mr. and Mrs. Morrison, but somehow she knew in her heart that she was exactly where she was meant to be—in this wild, amazing place with its strange, hostile people.

"Everything," her father had told her, "happens for a reason."

Martine couldn't for the life of her imagine what that

reason could possibly be, and right now she didn't care. She just knew that she needed a friend.

Outside, the wind slapped and banged around the house and the thunder cracked as if a thousand boulders were breaking across the heavens. Lightning split the sky. Martine gasped. A white giraffe was standing beside the water hole and it was looking straight at her! For a split second, their eyes locked, the small, sad girl and the slender young giraffe, and then the sky went dark. Martine pressed her face to the glass, desperate to see the white giraffe again, but it was impossible. There was no moon and the rain was coming down in sheets.

Martine felt so crushed she could hardly breathe. It was like getting the best present you could dream of—a pony, say—and then having it snatched away again before you even had a minute to enjoy it. It was almost too much for her to bear.

She tried to pull herself together. Had she seen the white giraffe or hadn't she? Could it have been a trick of the light? From this distance, there'd been something almost ghostly about it. In the lightning's blue flicker, it had had a phosphorescent glow. But when she relived the instant their eyes had met, she was certain. The white giraffe was out there. It had looked at her as though it were looking *for* her.

Martine had a sudden urge to rush out into the game park and find the shy creature. She knew there could be terrible consequences. She had been forbidden from ever going into the game reserve by herself, and not even Tendai would risk going in on foot after dark. Snakes, scorpions, lions, buffaloes, and even leopards were all on the prowl at night, and many of them would be out hunting. Martine was well aware that if she disobeyed the order, she could be attacked or gored or worse.

For a long time she sat at the window trying to decide what to do. She couldn't stop thinking about the white giraffe.

At last, she made up her mind. She took off the shorts she'd changed into after school and put on her jeans, boots, and navy blue school Windbreaker. Behind the bookcase, she'd concealed the carved wooden box Mr. Morrison had given to her. She removed her flashlight and knife and put them in her back pocket. At the door of her bedroom, she listened. The only sound was the slowing rain, muffled on the thickly thatched roof.

As silently as she could, she tiptoed down the stairs. The timber boards were old and with every creak Martine fully expected to hear her grandmother's enraged shriek or feel her hand on her shoulder. But nothing stirred.

When she reached the kitchen she stood for several minutes, breathing deeply and taking comfort in the reassuring hum of the fridge. Then she unlocked the kitchen door. There was something very final about the click it made as it swung shut behind her. She checked her watch.

It was one minute past midnight.

9

Out in the garden, the storm had slowed to a drizzle. Confronted with the sights and smells of the African night, Martine's courage almost deserted her. Had her grandmother's bedroom light not come on right at that very moment, she would have rushed back inside. But it did. Martine decided that if she had a choice between her grandmother and a hungry lion, she'd rather take her chances with the lion.

The air was perfume-sweet with the scent of fallen mangoes and gardenia blossoms. Martine set off blindly through the dripping trees in the general direction of the game park gate. The one useful thing she'd overheard during her investigations the previous week had been

Tendai telling her grandmother the new code for the padlock. She'd made a point of committing the numbers to memory. When her hands touched the cold metal gate, she felt for the heavy chain that bound it and the lock that secured it. Only then did she switch on her flashlight and enter the numbers on the wet dial. The padlock clicked open! Martine stared down at it, unable to believe that it had been so easy. She realized then that she'd been secretly hoping all along that something would happen to prevent her from going into the game reserve. She glanced over her shoulder. Once more, the house stood in darkness. Whatever happened now, there was no turning back.

Martine stepped through the gate and stifled a cry of terror. Two red eyes glared at her. The bushes shook violently and a waterbuck sprang up so close to Martine that its fur actually brushed her. With a shake of its horns, it bounded away into the blackness.

Martine's heart smacked wildly against her rib cage. She tried to imagine what Tendai would do in a similar situation. Not that he was likely to be in a similar situation, but if he were, she was sure that everything would be about staying calm and thinking clearly. Focus, she thought. I have to focus. I *can* do this.

More than anything in the world, she wanted to find the white giraffe. Why, she wasn't sure; she just knew she had to do it. And as frightened as she was, just doing something for herself and rebelling, even in a small way, against the stifling atmosphere of her grandmother's house, made her feel good.

The beam from her flashlight picked out the path that led down to the water hole, where the frogs were competing in a noisy chorus. Blue lightning shuddered over the mountains on the far horizon. Martine set off as quickly as she dared, trying to avoid the puddles. Even so, her jeans were soon soaked through. In places the grass was taller than she was, and cold droplets drenched her hair and ran down her neck.

As she walked, unseen creatures slithered and scurried and hopped away through the undergrowth. Martine tried not to imagine the worst. She wasn't sure which she was most scared of, snakes and creepy-crawlies or man-eating carnivores, but she fervently hoped that she didn't meet any of them. After what seemed an age, the temperature dropped and she saw she'd reached the water's edge. She tried to pinpoint the exact spot where she had seen the giraffe. She was pretty sure it had been beside the old gum tree that stood, like a startled skeleton, on the left bank of the water hole.

As if sensing danger, the frogs fell silent. Tendrils of mist hovered over the water and the night air was laden with threat. Martine quelled the butterflies in her stomach. She'd come too far to go back now. She lifted her flashlight and shined it into the surrounding bush. Nothing moved. Not a mouse, not a lion, not even a bird. Disappointment hit her like a blow. What had she been thinking? A mythical giraffe! She'd risked her life in pursuit of a fairy tale and now she had to try to get home in one piece.

Sheer instinct warned Martine something was behind her. The same sixth sense told her to turn around very, very slowly. A Cape cobra was coiled in the mud barely six feet away from her, hood spread wide, swaying in the yellow light. Martine recognized it immediately as one of the most poisonous snakes in Africa. Its golden coloring was unmistakable. So was the band around its throat.

The cobra's lips parted and its black tongue flickered out evilly. Martine dropped her flashlight in panic. It rolled behind a boulder and dimmed to a faint glow.

Then it went out.

In the split second before she was plunged into darkness, Martine saw the cobra draw back its head to strike. Helplessly, she waited for its lethal bite.

It never came. Instead, a pale blur exploded from the trees. There was a hideous hissing sound and the flash of flying hooves. The last thing Martine saw before she crumpled to the ground was the white giraffe.

Something was tickling Martine's face. Something that blew warm, sweet air reminiscent of a freshly mown lawn on a summer's day in England. Or strawberries at Wimbledon. Or the rose garden in Greenwich Park in London, which she had visited one spring on a school trip.

There was something else in the scent too, something wild and exotic and . . . African.

Africa!

Martine suddenly came to and realized that she was not dozing in the hammock in her garden in safe, suburban England. She had illicitly entered a South African game reserve in the middle of the night, and something was sniffing at her and possibly preparing to eat her. Cautiously, she opened one eye. A pair of liquid-black eyes framed by impossibly long lashes stared down at her.

"You saved my life," she said.

The white giraffe drew back with a nervous snort. It gave a half rear, like a horse, and retreated to a safe distance. Martine climbed carefully to her feet. The white giraffe towered over her. The sky had cleared a little and in the dim light of the watery moon, Martine could see it was an immensely beautiful creature. Its coat shimmered like sunlit snow and it was patterned all over with patches of silver tinged with cinnamon.

She reached out her hand to it and it wheeled around and made as if to flee before sliding to a halt, breathing hard and shaking. The wildlife book in her room had explained that although giraffes are basically very gentle creatures, they are quite capable of using their long front legs to kick with force if they feel threatened. But something told Martine that this particular giraffe would never hurt her.

She reached out her hand again and took a couple of steps toward it. "It's all right," she said soothingly. "It's all right. I only want to stroke you, not to harm you."

This time the giraffe stood still. When her fingers made contact with its skin, it quivered with fear, but didn't move away. Martine felt a tingle of electricity run up her arm—the same tingle she'd felt when Grace had put a hand on her forehead. In that instant, she had a strange sense she knew exactly what the animal was thinking. She knew, for example, without having any idea why, that his name was Jeremiah—Jemmy for short. And she knew that Jemmy was lonely. Every bit as lonely as she was.

"I'm alone too," Martine confided to the giraffe. "Five weeks ago, I lost everything I loved in a fire in England. Now I live with my grandmother who doesn't want me, and go to a school where I don't fit in."

The white giraffe watched her warily. He didn't respond. Instead he sidled restlessly out of range so she could no longer touch him. Perhaps, thought Martine, he was waiting for a sign that he could trust her. And who could blame him? If she wanted to get close to him, the first thing she was going to have to do was to prove to him that she was a friend. But how?

Then it came to her. In England, her mum and dad had had a poster in their bedroom of a dove being released into a sunset. On it was written: *If you love something, set it free. If it comes back to you, it's yours. If it doesn't, it never was.* Martine could remember as if it were yesterday her mum's voice reading it aloud to her, and then saying with a smile, "Isn't that wonderful, Martine? And it's true. The more you love something, the more you have to give it space to find its own way in the world. That way you'll know that if it comes back to you, it's because it truly cares for you."

As miraculous as it was that she'd found the white giraffe, Martine knew she had to walk away from him. She took a last lingering look at him. Her heart ached, as if she were losing a friend she'd only just made, but somehow she knew they'd meet again. For reasons she didn't fully understand, she felt as if their souls were already entwined.

"Thank you for saving my life, Jeremiah," she said, adding hopefully: "See you soon."

With that, she began picking her way through the mud to the grassy track. She was a bit hazy on the fate of the cobra, but she hoped it was either extremely dead or cowering in its burrow. She wasn't sure she would survive another encounter with it.

She was almost there when a twig snapped like a firecracker in the darkness. Martine had never been much of an athlete, but she was on the verge of sprinting like an Olympian for the house when she spotted a reflection in the water. The white giraffe was following her! She pretended to walk on. The mirrored giraffe stepped gracefully after her, his white-gold coat and silvery patches flowing across the steely water like an elegant ghost. Martine paused. The white giraffe paused. She continued. The white giraffe continued. She swung around abruptly.

The giraffe slid to an awkward stop in the mud. He contemplated Martine from his great height. He seemed inquisitive now, rather than afraid. Martine craned her neck and tried to read his expression. She decided that it was like gazing into the eyes of the wisest creature on earth and the most innocent at the same time. Her overwhelming impression was one of gentleness.

She waited to see what the giraffe would do. At first nothing happened, but then he lowered his head, inch by inch, until his slender nose was close enough to touch. Again Martine smelled his clean, newly cut grass scent. She longed to put her palm against his satiny white jaw, but she forced herself to stay still.

Then something extraordinary happened. The giraffe rested his head on Martine's shoulder and made a low, musical fluttering sound.

For one perfect moment they stood there—the small girl and the white giraffe—mirrored in the moonlit water. It was only a minute, but it was long enough for the emotions and confusion of the past few weeks to leave Martine in a rush and suffuse her with a feeling of contentment. She knew then that she'd come home.

A lion roared. In the eerily quiet aftermath of the storm, the sound blasted through the night as though the beast was about to pounce on them. Martine and the giraffe were in full flight—in opposite directions—before either of them had given the matter any conscious thought. There were no good-byes. By the time she'd reached the safety of the garden, the white giraffe had vanished as if he had never been.

10

Back in her room, Martine fell into an exhausted sleep. When her alarm woke her at six, she forced herself to spring out of bed, pull on her wet, muddy jeans, and rush out into the early-morning sunlight, pausing only to splash icy water on her face. She knew she had to find an excuse for the state of her clothes. By the time her grandmother emerged to feed Shaka at six thirty, Martine was on her knees in the vegetable garden, weeding furiously.

Gwyn Thomas could hardly believe her eyes. "Whatever are you doing, child?" she asked. "You're absolutely filthy."

"I'm just trying to clear the weeds away from these carrots," Martine said brightly. "I've been doing some thinking and I've realized that I need to start helping you a bit more around the house."

"Well . . ." said her grandmother. "Well, I . . . well, thank you, Martine."

Neither of them mentioned the fight of the evening before. However, Gwyn Thomas, who generally served up an unchanging breakfast of boiled eggs and toast, made Martine a special treat of fresh papaya and mango, a South African porridge called jungle oats, and homemade bread with Cape gooseberry jam. Martine was just savoring the last incredible bite when Alex du Preez's gray Land Rover came roaring up the drive.

Martine scowled. She'd only met the game warden once, but she'd disliked him on sight. He was what her mum would have described as a "snakeoil salesman," over-familiar and full of insincere patter. He gave her the creeps. She couldn't believe he had any empathy with animals.

His freckled face, topped by a shock of strawberry blond hair, appeared at the front door. "Good morning, Mrs. Thomas, Martine," he said breezily. "How are you ladies on this beautiful day?"

"Very well, thank you, Alex," said her grandmother, smiling. "What brings you here so early?"

"Ma'am, I'm just heading into Storm Crossing to buy some zebra feed. I know you've got a lot to do, so I thought it might be helpful if I gave Martine a lift to school today."

"Why Alex, it most certainly would. I've got the vet arriving first thing to check on Shaka and the two buffaloes who had that awful fight yesterday, and a party of twenty-four Swedish businessmen coming at ten. I really do appreciate your thoughtfulness. Wait a moment while I get her packed lunch."

Martine's heart sank. She trailed out of the door after Alex's stocky frame.

Once on the road, Alex started up a stream of boring chatter in his thick South African accent. Martine, who wanted nothing more than to lose herself in a dreamy reverie about her encounter with the white giraffe the previous night—he'd followed her, and rested his satiny head on her shoulder!—gave him a series of one-word answers, but it didn't seem to discourage him.

"You're a smart little thing, aren't you?" he said as they stopped at the single traffic light in Storm Crossing. "I bet you're much better than I was at schoolwork."

"I'm eleven," Martine said rudely. "Don't talk to me like I'm a five-year-old."

A sly look came across Alex's face. "Okay," he said. "If that's the way you want to play it. You haven't by any chance come across a white giraffe at Sawubona, have you, Martine?"

Martine did her best to keep the shock from showing on her face. "The white giraffe doesn't exist," she answered. "Everybody knows that."

Alex put his hand in his pocket and took out Martine's precious flashlight. He threw it on the cracked leather seat beside her. She itched to pick it up but didn't dare.

Alex gave a cruel laugh. "Be like that, then." He put the

65

flashlight back in his pocket. "The thing is, Martine, the white giraffe, if it did exist, would be very, very valuable. Your grandmother, for instance, would really benefit from the sale of such an animal. I mean, we're talking about tens of thousands of dollars here, not chicken feed. Now, I would hate to think that you would jeopardize the future of everyone on Sawubona by poking around in things that are none of your business. How do you think your grandmother would feel about that?"

Martine was livid. How dare he talk about Jemmy as if he were just another animal to be hunted down and turned into money? She was pretty sure her grandmother didn't know about his ideas either.

"And how do you think my grandmother would feel if she knew about *your* little secret?" she retaliated, just to test him.

Alex's blue eyes blazed. He pulled into the school, slammed on the brakes, and reached across her to open the door. "My girl," he said, "you are playing with fire now." He smiled grimly. "And you know what happens to people who play with fire . . ."

Martine tried to be strong until she was out of the jeep, but as soon as she turned away from him the tears began to pour down her face.

His laughter followed her all the way across the school yard.

11

It is possible that Martine would have continued to settle into Caracal School and, in spite of her shyness, would eventually have made friends, but on her third Sunday in Africa something happened to change everything. It all started with a school outing to the Kirstenbosch National Botanical Gardens in Cape Town, a place, Miss Volkner told them, of "incomparable marvels when it comes to the plant kingdom."

Throughout the week Miss Volkner had drummed them into a state of excitement about it, promising them a weekend treat they would never forget, during which they would explore things like the Fragrance and Medicine Gardens, and enjoy a special picnic at the foot of Table Mountain while watching a world-renowned African band.

Martine had looked forward to the trip with some trepidation and was very relieved when, a short time after boarding the bus at Caracal at noon on Sunday, she found she was enjoying herself. There was a good atmosphere on the way into Cape Town and some of the children were telling jokes and singing. "Why was six cross?" Sherilyn Meyer asked Martine. "Because seven ate nine! Eight, ate, do you get it?"

Martine was laughing harder than she actually meant to when she caught sight of Ben—alone, as usual, at the back of the bus. She looked away guiltily. Maybe today she would try to find a way to speak to him. To distract herself, she reflected on the conversation with Alex two days previously. The way he had talked, anyone would think there was a conspiracy at Sawubona to preserve the secret of the white giraffe until it could be captured and sold for a king's ransom. And yet both Tendai and Gwyn Thomas had insisted to her that it was a myth. Either Alex knew more than they did, or they were lying.

Martine thought again about her encounter with the white giraffe; about the moment when she first saw him towering above her, shimmering white like sun on snow, with patches of silver tinged with cinnamon. A shiver of excitement went through her. Nothing on earth would stop her from seeing Jemmy again—no storm, no lock, no game warden, no threat. Nothing was more important than the white giraffe.

The squeal of the bus brakes interrupted Martine's thoughts. They were entering Gate Two at Kirstenbosch Botanical Gardens. As she waited to get off, she stole a glance at Ben. He didn't seem to have noticed that the bus had stopped. He was staring out at the paradise of trees and flowers and Table Mountain rising into the blue sky behind it, and his face was alive with anticipation.

At the Kirstenbosch Nature Study School, smiling staff greeted them with fruit juice and a lecture on the Botanical Gardens, which had been established in 1913 and were spread over a massive 1,300 acres. After that, they were split into three groups of eight. Two of the groups were to explore Kirstenbosch with an education officer, but Martine's group, which consisted of four members of the Five Star Gang (everyone except Pieter), plus Sherilyn, a big sporty boy called Jake, and Ben, was to be led by Miss Volkner, who had done a special course at the center to enable her to guide them.

Their first stop was to be the Fragrance Garden. They set off over the manicured lawns, where tourists picnicked and guinea fowl hovered hopefully for tidbits, crossing a bubbling brook along the way. It looked innocent enough, but it had a brutal and bloody history as an escape route of slaves in the days when the British ruled the Cape colony. "Legend has it that one slave who escaped here was eaten by a leopard, and all that was found of him was his skeleton," Miss Volkner told them. "Ever since then, this has been known as Skeleton Stream and the area above it as Skeleton Gorge.

"The older forest beside it is called *Donker Gat*, Afrikaans for Dark Corner." She added for effect, "Many a child has been lost up there."

An echo passed through Martine—a sort of chill. Her eyes followed Miss Volkner's pointing finger up the forbidding slopes of Table Mountain, where forests of yellowwood and ironwood sprawled in a dense green carpet. The scene looked familiar, as if she'd seen it before in a photograph. Goose bumps rose on her arms. Less than an hour ago the sky had been clear, with only a few wisps of cloud over the mountain, but already the day was turning ugly. They had been warned about the unpredictability of the weather. For no particular reason, Martine suddenly felt apprehensive.

The Fragrance and Medicinal Gardens were wonderlands of aromatic plants and healing herbs, but Martine found it difficult to concentrate. At the Dell, they drank from an ice-cold spring in a bird-shaped bath and then it was on to the Cycad Ampitheater, where Miss Volkner explained that the palm-like cycads were actually living fossils that were around in the time of the dinosaurs. "Some of them are two hundred million years old," she said. "Can you believe that? Two hundred *million* years old."

The final stage of their journey was the Fynbos Walk on the lower slopes of the mountain. Fynbos was one of the world's six plant kingdoms and was unique to the Cape Region. It consisted of heathery-type bushes like the bright red fire heath, silver trees, reeds, lilies, and pink, velvety proteas, which were South Africa's national flower. Sprawling alongside the winding paths in a blaze of color, it made for a spectacular display. When they reached the Protea Garden Miss Volkner showed them the orange-headed nodding pincushion flower, a favorite nectar of the sugar birds. Just then, her beeper went off. She checked it with a grimace, the wind whipping her curly hair.

"Okay, everyone, pay attention," she called. "One of the other children has suffered an allergic reaction to a bee sting and I'm urgently needed back at the Nature Study School. It would be a shame for you to miss out on seeing the sugar birds feed, so I'm going to trust you to stay here quietly and wait for them. Under no circumstances is anyone to go wandering off. Luke and Lucy, as prefects, I'm putting you in charge. If I'm not back in the next twenty minutes, follow the signs to the concert area and I'll meet you there."

As soon as Miss Volkner was out of sight, mayhem erupted. No one apart from Martine seemed to have the slightest interest in seeing the sugar birds feed. There were a few other visitors in the Protea Garden, but the noise of the children soon drove them away. Martine decided that now would be a good time to try to talk to Ben. She walked through the flower beds in search of him, but he was nowhere to be seen.

"Where's Ben?" she asked Lucy.

"Who knows," the blond girl said disinterestedly. "Probably hugging a tree or something."

Sherilyn interrupted: "What's happening to the sky?"

Eight heads tipped upward. The wispy cloud had become a vaporous gray blanket. It had consumed the top half of the mountain and was sliding furiously down the cliffs toward Kirstenbosch, driven by the wind. But the really creepy part was the sky, which boiled with an odd violet light. It looked less like a storm was approaching than some weather phenomenon, like a tornado or a tempest.

"Please can we go back now, guys? It's freezing," whined Sherilyn, but the prospect of extreme weather had added to the atmosphere of silliness, and the other children started chasing moths through the Protea Garden.

The sound of marimbas, conga drums, and African voices rising in exquisite harmony came to them on the gusting wind. The band had started playing.

A flash of memory seared Martine's brain. It was the music from her dream, she was sure of it! That explained it. That's why Kirstenbosch was so familiar. Her dream was becoming reality. And this was the exact scene! The looming gray mountain, the plum-colored light, the swallowing cloud, and the children chasing moths through the proteas. Any minute now, someone would go: "Hey, look what I found . . ."

"Hey!" Luke was standing by a stack of wooden stakes of the sort used to create fences. His voice was excited. "Look what I found."

The others rushed to his side, Martine included, although warning bells were clanging like a sixty-piece orchestra in her head.

An Egyptian goose lay on the ground. It was a large bird with reddish-brown and white wings, but one of those wings hung broken and its webbed feet curled limply at its breast. It stared up at the peering faces with one red eye. Though it flapped feebly, it was unable to move. Luke scooped the bird up and it honked hoarsely in protest.

"I bet it's been attacked by a fox. Miss Volkner said there were foxes around."

"Put it down, Luke," Lucy snapped at her brother. "It's probably diseased."

"Yeah, Luke, it's dirty," agreed Jake.

Martine tried to speak, but no sound came out.

"Maybe we should put it out of its misery," Luke suggested. "You know, hit it over the head or something."

Jake laughed. "How 'bout a *braai*, a nice little barbecue. We can put it on a spit. Should be enough to go around."

Martine found her voice. She said tearfully: "Please leave it alone. Please don't hurt it."

"Ah, poor little English girl," jeered Luke. "Cwying like a baby. You want it? Here, have it. Catch."

He launched the goose at Martine, who flailed blindly for the brown blur and, unprepared for the weight of it, tripped and toppled over backward. Somehow she managed to hold on to it through her fall. She struggled into a kneeling position with the goose still cradled in her arms, her face flushed scarlet with anger and embarrassment. The other kids burst out laughing.

"Did you see that?" Jake crowed delightedly. "That was priceless." He mimicked Martine's windmill arms and plaintive voice. "*Pleeease* don't hurt it."

Caught up in the madness of the moment, none of the children noticed that Martine had closed her eyes and was trembling violently. She was remembering the goose in her dream. That goose too had had a tiny pulse beating in its throat and brown silken feathers that were warm to the touch. This bird's eyes slid shut as she watched it.

Martine's first thought was that she had to try to save it. Her second was, *How?* Then a voice in her head, a voice she recognized as Grace's, said, "You know what to do, chile." And right at that instant Martine realized that she *did* know what to do; that she had always known, all her life. Her hands ceased trembling and heated up to the point where they were practically glowing. After a few seconds the Egyptian goose jerked and its eyelids flickered. She loosened her palms. It shook out its wings and flew into the darkening sky.

The world swam into focus again.

Her classmates were staring at her with a mixture of fear, horror, and disbelief. The color had drained from Luke's face and he was backing away from her as if she were possessed. "Hey, how did you do that? What are you, some kind of witch?"

Martine was just as bewildered as he was. In the instant when her palms were at their hottest, she'd felt a power as ancient as the earth go through her like an ocean wave, and had seen, in a puff of smoke, a procession of what she could only imagine were spirits—Africans in antelope masks and rhinoceroses breathing fire. Dazed and shaky, all she could think was: So this is it. *This* is the gift.

"What is it?" Luke was yelling at her. "Is it black magic? *Voodoo?*"

"Maybe she's an *umthakathi*," accused Xhosa. "That's the Zulu word for a wizard or witch, someone who bewitches others or casts spells on them. Be careful, she might change into a bat or a bird."

Martine stuttered, "I'm not an um . . . I'm not a w-witch."

"You know, in South Africa, some people say that there is only one thing to do with an *umthakathi*," Xhosa said. "They must be eliminated. Otherwise they will do evil things."

Martine cast a desperate glance down the mountainside, hoping to see the sturdy figure of Miss Volkner coming to call them for the picnic. But no one was there.

"You wouldn't," she said in a small voice.

Nobody answered, but Jake took a threatening step toward her. Martine made a move toward the path that led to the main center, but the other children cut her off.

She looked beseechingly at Lucy, but the blond girl was wearing the same supercilious expression she adopted whenever anyone spoke about Ben.

That's when she knew that they were serious.

Martine spun on her heel and fled into the twilight,

screaming for help as she went, but the band drowned out her cries. She ran down a short hill, over Nursery Stream and into an evergreen forest. Only then did she realize her mistake. Ahead of her was a daunting wall of 330 steps. She halted, panting, unsure what to do, but the clattering of feet and cries of her pursuers on the wooden bridge jolted her into action. She flew up the steps as if the hounds of hell were on her trail. With every one, the agony in her legs increased and her breath burned like acid in her chest. At the top was a road but no signs. Martine knew that she wouldn't be able to keep going for much longer, so she plunged into the wilderness of yellowwood trees. Better to be lost than to be caught.

Once in the greeny dark of the forest, she could no longer hear the noise of the city, just the tinkle of streams and the faint whisper and twitter of birds, bats, and snakes high up in the canopy. Clouds oozed through the branches and hung above the narrow path. Higher and higher Martine climbed. When she paused to suck air into her fiery lungs, she caught a panoramic glimpse of the hazy city miles below and of the Botanical Gardens, now in miniature like a village made of LEGOs, with toys for cars. Behind her, she heard the shouts of the children as they entered the forest. She dragged herself forward, wild asparagus thorns hooking her ankles, but even as she did so, she knew she couldn't run anymore. Her legs were too rubbery to support her.

All at once, an arm shot out from behind a tree and she was yanked sideways into a hollow. Martine opened her mouth to scream, just as she had in that long-ago dream, but she was so startled and breathless that all she could manage was a small whimper before crumpling into a bed of leaves. She steeled herself for a blow, but none came. Squinting up through the misty darkness, she made out the face of her captor. Ben! He wrapped his arms protectively around her and, despite being small, he was warm and solid and she could feel the thud, thud, thud of his heart.

"Martine," called Jake in a singsong voice, "where *are* you?" Leaves crunched under the feet of the gang as they hurried by.

Ben put a finger to his lips. He reached down and picked up a handful of small stones and threw them as far as he could. They made a series of popping noises as they landed, like tiny bullets.

Luke shouted, "Over there! Come on, everyone."

There were whooping noises and the cracking of fallen branches as they pounded away down the track.

Martine became aware that Ben was shaking with silent laughter. He laughed so hard that he doubled over and had to hold his stomach.

"What is it?" Martine whispered. "What's so funny?"

Ben straightened up long enough to point at a sign propped against the tree. The base of it was still damp with fresh soil. On it was written:

WARNING: RAW COMPOST TANK
DO NOT ENTER

12

Martine said nothing to her grandmother about the Botanical Gardens drama, which had ended with six of her pursuers falling into a stinking stew of fermenting horse manure, rotting fruit, decaying leaves, and squashed bugs. Sherilyn had escaped because she hadn't been able to keep up with the others, but the search party who found them had discovered her babbling incomprehensibly after an encounter with a lynx cat with glowing yellow eyes. Miss Volkner was apoplectic with fury. She was particularly enraged that no one would own up to what had happened. Even Mrs. Rathmore lost her sense of humor and said that if it wasn't that she thought the six had been punished enough by missing out on the band and picnic, and being mercilessly teased on the bus to Storm Crossing (where they were made to sit at the back, hungry and scowling, like the broken survivors of a mud-wrestling competition), they would have spent the rest of the term cutting the school fields with nail scissors.

What nobody could figure out was how Martine and Ben came to be sitting quietly on a picnic blanket near the band, enjoying hot buttered corn and big slabs of milk tart, a vanilla custard pie. Miss Volkner had her suspicions and told them she'd be keeping a very close eye on them, but it was the wrath of the Five Star kids Martine feared most.

"We'll get you for this," Scott Henderson had hissed as he boarded the bus, dripping, and somehow she didn't doubt that they would.

Fortunately for Martine, ever since her grandmother had found her helping out in the garden the morning after the fight, a truce had been declared at home. So much so that Gwyn Thomas finally relented and allowed Martine to go with Tendai when he did his rounds of the reserve the following weekend. He picked her up in the jeep at four thirty on Saturday morning, when dawn was nothing but a smudge in a star-speckled sky, and drove her to Sawubona's highest point, an escarpment densely covered in aloes, proteas, and a shrub that smelled like curry. Cacti clung to the lichen-plastered rocks.

The track that led to the top of the escarpment was badly eroded and treacherous, so Tendai and Martine walked the last part of the way, and the sky was etched with fiery hues when they reached their destination. While Tendai unpacked their breakfast, Martine made herself comfortable on a boulder still warm from the heat of the previous day. Far below her was the biggest dam on Sawubona. As the sun rose and her eyes became accustomed to the honeyed light, Martine could make out herds of buffalo, springboks, and elephants drifting down to the water. White egrets watched from the trees like the stiff paper birds of Japanese origami.

Martine thought that she had never breathed in purer air, seen a lovelier view, or heard any choir more amazing than the singing of the birds that morning. She wished her mum and dad could have been there to share it, but it made her feel good to think that her mum had probably visited this spot and watched the same sunrise.

Tendai made a small fire and brewed up a pot of condensed milk–sweetened tea. He handed Martine some hot African bread made with maize meal, cooked in the coals in tightly wrapped banana leaves, and they munched contentedly and watched the animals in the valley below.

After a while, Martine said, "Tendai, can I ask you a question?"

"Yebo."

"Sure?"

"Yebo."

"How did you get the scar on your face?"

Tendai laughed, but it was a bitter laugh devoid of his usual good humor. "It was a long time ago, little one. Too long ago to be important. I was an angry young man, that's all."

Martine could tell that he didn't want to talk about it, but curiosity got the better of her. "Did an animal attack you, or did you get into a fight?"

Tendai unbuttoned his khaki shirt and Martine clapped a hand to her mouth. His back and broad chest were criss-crossed with fifty or sixty thick, raised scars. It was as if someone or something had tried to cut him into a million pieces.

"What animal would do this?" he said harshly. "No, little one, animals might scratch you, or bite you, or even rip you apart in hunger or in fear, but only a man can crush you inside, in your heart, for no reason other than the color of your skin."

Martine swallowed.

Tendai had a faraway expression on his face. When he began to talk, it was as if he were seeing something that had happened in another land, in another lifetime. He had been twelve years old when his parents had moved from a peaceful village in the Drakensberg Mountains to the notorious township of Soweto, near Johannesburg, in search of work.

"For many years," Tendai recalled, "it was as if the devil himself had moved to Soweto and turned it into hell. But it was a hell just for black people. Whole families lived in corrugated iron shacks without toilets or running water.

81

When darkness fell, we burned fires to keep away the cock- roaches and rats, and armed gangs roamed the streets." He stopped. "Perhaps I should not be telling you this. Your grandmother might not like it."

Martine got up off her boulder and moved nearer to him. "Please, Tendai," she said. "I want to know."

In spite of the hardship of life in Soweto, Tendai consid- ered himself luckier than most. His mother was a trained teacher and she'd helped him study in their shack. He worked hard and dreamed of one day being able to re- turn to the mountains and buy a farm of his own. When he was seventeen, he managed to get a job as a clerk at a railway station. He was prouder than he had ever been in his life. There was only one problem. Every day he walked five miles to work and almost every day he was stopped by police wanting to check his papers. At that time it was illegal for a non-white—a man of color—to go anywhere without identification.

"One policeman in particular, it was as if he hated me without even knowing me. Sometimes I felt that he was just waiting to catch me out."

Martine realized she was trembling. "And did he?"

Tendai nodded. "He caught me without my papers. My mother had washed my shirt and had forgotten to return the papers to the pocket after it was dry. This policeman began to strike me with his stick and shout at me for having no identification. When I reminded him that he had checked it many times before, he called me names. Then he tore my shirt. I had kept my temper all this time, but when he tore my shirt—without it, I couldn't go to my job—I'm sorry to say I punched him as hard as I could."

After that, Tendai remembered very little. When he regained consciousness, he was in a prison hospital, covered in the welts of a *sjambok*, a whip made of rhinoceros hide. When he was released from jail nine months later, he found that his parents had been taken away by the authorities. He never saw them again. At eighteen he was a broken man, living rough on the streets of Johannesburg, when Grace sent for him.

"It was Grace who taught me that the best revenge is forgiveness," Tendai said. "Sometimes the thing that hurts your enemies most is to see that you are not like them. Grace introduced me to your grandfather, who changed my life. He believed in a South Africa where men of all colors are equal. Not everybody does."

"Why not?" asked Martine. For some reason the face of Alex du Preez, as he threatened her, swam into her mind.

"I don't know, little one," Tendai said tiredly. "I just don't know."

They packed up the breakfast things, threw sand over the coals, and headed back down the escarpment. The grass was still wet with dew, but the early-morning sun was already hot on their skin. As they walked, Tendai gave Martine her first lesson in bushcraft. He picked an aloe leaf and showed her how to squeeze a gel from it that could soothe burns or rashes, heal wounds, or calm itching.

That was impressive, but the aloe couldn't even begin to compete with the marula tree, which was practically a one-stop pharmacy. Not only did its golden yellow fruit soothe stomachaches, Tendai told her, but it had four times as much vitamin C as an orange. Its leaves were great for dressing wounds or treating insect bites, and its bark reduced inflammation. And that wasn't all. The pit of the marula fruit contained an oil that the Africans prized as nose or ear drops, or lit in its shell as a natural candle. The Zulus even believed that if a person suffering from measles rose before dawn, went down to the tree without speaking to anyone, and bit the bark, he'd be cured.

Martine gazed around her in wonderment. With every passing day, she felt more and more that she belonged here. It was as if the landscape itself were creeping into her soul. She thought of it as a language. Every new bird call, every breath of wind, every new plant, and each fresh encounter she had with the local people or animals was like learning a new word. Put together, it made up the language of the bush. She hoped that if she studied hard enough, she'd be as fluent one day as Tendai was.

"Show me more," she urged him, and he did. He taught her how to identify a multi-layered orange mushroom that was delicious if it was roasted, and how to make a cone of leaves to trap dew or rainwater. He even showed her the "toilet paper" tree, which had soft fronds that came in handy if you were far from home and caught short!

Best of all, he taught her how to make a natural compass. First, he selected a straight stick about three feet long. He pushed it into the ground in an area away from any grass or vegetation, so that it cast a clear shadow.

"When you're sure that the stick is standing up nicely, you mark the tip of the shadow with your finger or a twig," he told Martine. "Wait fifteen minutes. When the shadow moves, mark the tip again. Draw a straight line through the two marks, like so. This will be your east-west line. If you now put your left foot on the first shadow mark and your right foot on the second one, you will be facing roughly north. There are more accurate ways of doing it, but for you, I think, this is the easiest."

Martine could have gone on listening to bush lessons all day long, but she knew Tendai had work to do, so she thanked him and they continued down the escarpment. The path was overgrown and their way was frequently blocked by cacti and massive boulders. Once, when Martine was about to jump from a rock onto a soft pile of leaves, Tendai's arm shot out and he pushed her back so hard that she slipped and grazed her bare knee. She was opening her mouth to ask, a little crossly, what he was doing, when she saw Tendai's somber face. Lying in the leaves, completely camouflaged by the browns, grays, and yellows, were a dozen baby Berg adders. Tendai assured her they were every bit as poisonous as their mother.

Martine was shaken. It was the second time in less than two weeks that her life had been saved. "What would have happened to me if I'd been bitten?"

Tendai smiled. "But you weren't."

"But what would have happened if I had been?"

The Zulu refused to answer. "With any snake bite, you must stay as calm and quiet as possible. Try to identify the snake and walk slowly to get help."

Urine, it turned out, was an excellent antiseptic and the perfect thing to use if there was no water nearby when a cobra spat in your eye. Martine tried to imagine herself calmly peeing into a cup or even her hand and then using it to wash out her eyes. Ugh, she thought, and shuddered as she remembered her close shave with the cobra the other evening. She resolved to give snakes a wide berth in the future.

Tendai saw her expression and erupted into laughter. "Don't worry, little one. Snakes usually do their best to avoid people and seldom bite unless they are cornered or threatened."

"Mmm," murmured Martine doubtfully.

13

When they reached the jeep, Tendai put the breakfast things in the cab and took out his rifle. They set off on foot across the valley. The sun was so searing that even the earth smelled baked and the sky was as blue as a kingfisher's wing. At this hour of day there was no shade to speak of, but the lacy-leafed thorn trees were alive with bees, cooing doves, and crested gray louries, which her grandmother and Tendai referred to as "go-away birds" because that's what they seemed to shout at potential predators. These were the sounds Martine had come to associate with Africa.

She stuck close to Tendai, who walked with his hand on the trigger of his rifle, alert for elephants, buffaloes, and lions, the most unpredictable animals in the reserve. He noticed everything. He showed Martine a nest of hoopoe bird babies, a comical chameleon, and the spoor of a female leopard and two cubs. He could even tell how big the cubs were and how fast the little family had been traveling.

The more Tendai talked, the more obvious it was that he knew Sawubona like he knew his own heart. Martine felt safe with him. With his gravelly voice and patient way of explaining things, he reminded her of her father.

All at once, Tendai broke off. He made a clicking noise of irritation and took some pliers out of his pocket. They were in the valley to search for snares, wire nooses, or iron-jawed traps left by poachers, which strangled animals or broke their limbs and left them to die slowly. Martine watched him as he sprang a trap, almost invisible in the long grass, and cut the rusty wire binding it to a tree.

"I don't know what to do anymore," he said as they walked into the welcome cool of a grove of trees. "No matter how many snares I remove, they are always there the next day. And recently we've started to lose our big game as well. A lion and a buffalo have disappeared in the last month. I wish we could employ a guard, but money is very tight."

Listening to him, Martine began to feel frightened for Jeremiah. What if her giraffe (she'd already begun to think of Jemmy as *hers*) had his legs broken in a steel trap?

"Tendai . . . ?"

The Zulu put his finger to his lips. He indicated that she should creep forward quietly and crouch with him behind a tree. They sat motionless. After a few minutes, a magnificent kudu bull stepped gracefully into the clearing in front of them and stood in the dappled sunlight. He seemed to be listening for something. Martine thought that next to Jemmy he was the most gorgeous animal she had ever seen. He had spiral horns and almond-shaped eyes in a broad, fawn-colored face. Long silky white fur traced the line of his throat and delicate white stripes adorned his back, which was humped at the shoulder.

"He's amazing," she whispered to Tendai, who grinned down at her.

BANG!

A bullet ripped into the tree trunk above Tendai's head, simultaneously spraying him with splinters and terrifying Martine. Before they could move, a second bullet hit the kudu in the throat. Blood spurted from his neck in a fountain and he dropped to the ground and lay still. Martine screamed.

Alex came strolling through the trees, smoke rising from the tip of his rifle. His blond hair was standing up in sweaty spikes.

"Sorry about that, guys," he said. "The sight on my gun's been playing up. Lucky I missed you, hey! I was trying to hit that kudu over there. From where I was, it looked like it was caught in a snare."

Tendai was enraged. "There was nothing wrong with that kudu, nothing!" he shouted. "Where is the snare? What did you have to go and shoot it for?"

"What can I say?" Alex mused chirpily. "These things happen. At least it'll make good eating."

This incensed Tendai even more and the two men started to argue. Neither of them noticed Martine steal away and run as fast as she could to the fallen kudu. His eyes were glazed over and his lovely fawn coat was scarlet with pulsing blood. The rifle blast had left a big jagged hole in his white-bearded throat.

Martine bent down beside him. She was in a trance, just as she had been when she held the wild goose. Ordinarily, she would have been inconsolable at the mere idea of anyone shooting an animal, but today she didn't feel any sadness at all. Instead she felt charged with energy, as if the purest, most perfect electricity in the world was coursing through her veins. Her hands became boiling hot. She put them over the kudu's heart. There was a faint beat, already fading.

Martine thought fast. Shock and loss of blood had caused the kudu to lose consciousness and she knew from the first aid her dad had taught her that without emergency treatment he would be dead in minutes. But that didn't mean he couldn't be saved. The bullet had pierced the kudu's throat, passed straight through his windpipe, and made a clean exit. If Martine could stem the blood and heal his failing heart, then maybe, just maybe, the kudu would breathe again.

In the distance, she heard Alex snap sarcastically, "The trouble with you, Tendai, is you always put sentiment before business. A dead animal is not always a disaster, my friend. Sometimes it's just a furry bit of money."

Martine shut him out and put her hand over the hole in the kudu's throat. Blood bubbled through the gaps in her fingers. Every second counted. She scanned the area around her, desperately searching for something that could help to seal the wound. There was nothing but pale dirt, tufts of dry grass, and a big anthill. An anthill! Martine had a sudden flashback of Miss Volkner telling the class how the Shangaan tribe had once used soldier termites, which had very large mandibles or pincers, to "stitch up" wounds. What made it so effective, Miss Volkner had told them, was that the termites' saliva worked as a natural antiseptic.

"The down side," she'd added, with what Martine had thought was unnecessary relish, "is that, after the soldiers have locked their jaws, you have to rip their bodies off. That way, they won't be tempted to let go."

Martine had been squeamish about the decapitation of the poor termites at the time and, as she watched them making their way innocently home past her left knee, she didn't feel any better about it now. But she also knew she had to save the kudu.

The soldier termites were easy to spot. They had bulbous red heads on tiny cream bodies and their black mandibles waved in the air like weapons. As quick as a flash, she brought the edges of the wound together in a neat line, grabbed a passing soldier by the non-biting end and held its pincers to the pink flesh. It clamped down hard. Before she could think about it, Martine whipped off its rear. It worked! The soldier's black mandibles curved into the kudu's skin exactly like a stitch. She picked up another termite and did the same thing again, telling herself that at least it had died for a good cause. It hadn't just been stepped on by mistake or something. In under a minute, twenty termite heads sealed the wound as tightly as any surgeon could have done. Not a trickle of blood escaped.

Martine placed her hot hands over the kudu's dying heart and began pressing down every few seconds. Under her touch, the beat grew stronger and the kudu's skin became warm. When he opened his eyes and saw Martine, he appeared confused, but not frightened. He climbed to his feet shakily and, with a flick of his tail, bounded weakly away.

She watched him go, flooded with an indescribable feeling of joy. All she could think was: Dad would have been proud of me.

That's when she realized that somehow, without noticing it, she was finding her feet in her new world, and because of that, happiness was creeping up on her again. Three times in the last few weeks—saving the Egyptian goose, finding Jemmy, and now healing the kudu—she'd had to do things on her own, with nobody else's help, even when she was very, very scared, and each time something amazing had happened. And that made her trust herself more.

Even so, she was scared to look at the two men in case they'd witnessed what had just taken place. Fortunately, it seemed they hadn't. Alex had his back to her and Tendai's view was blocked by the game warden's body. They were still arguing. She used a tuft of grass and some spit to wipe the blood off her hands and walked over to them.

"Kudu's gone," she announced casually.

The men stopped ranting and stared at the spot where the kudu had been.

Tendai rubbed his eyes. He went a funny gray color. His gaze went from Martine to the clearing, then back again.

"Where's the kudu?" roared Alex. "*Where's the kudu?* It was dead. How the hell could it have moved?"

"He felt better," said Martine. "He decided that it wasn't a great idea to hang around while the sight on your gun isn't working."

Alex made a move toward her as if he were going to throttle her with his bare hands.

"*You* again," he snarled. "Remember what I told you. Be very, *very* careful. Next time you might not be so lucky." He turned to Tendai. "And as for you, just for the record, you should know that it's not the new South Africa on this game reserve."

He picked up his gun and stormed off into the trees.

Martine waited until she heard his truck speeding away.

"He could have killed you," she said.

The Zulu was sitting on the ground with his head in his hands. There were two ugly gashes on his face caused by ricocheting splinters. He lifted his head. "Please don't say anything to your grandmother." He didn't want to distress her unnecessarily.

"Tendai!"

"Please."

"Okay," Martine agreed unhappily.

They were silent for a minute. Then Tendai said: "My aunt was right, wasn't she, little one? You have the gift."

Martine didn't answer.

"The kudu," persisted Tendai. "It was dying. What did you do to it?"

"He was resting," said Martine. "The kudu was just resting."

And with that Tendai had to be satisfied.

14

The combination of Alex's bizarre behavior and the bone-crushing snares Tendai had destroyed in the valley had unnerved Martine so much that rather than waiting for the white giraffe to find her, as she'd promised herself she would, she became determined to find him again. For once, luck was on her side. Eight days after her outing with Tendai, a Sunday, her grandmother received a call to say that a close friend of hers had been rushed to the hospital. The hospital was in Somerset West, a couple of hours' drive away, and Gwyn Thomas would have to spend the night. She wanted to take Martine with her, but Martine convinced her that it would be much better if she stayed at Sawubona.

"I don't want to be tired for school in the morning."

"That's true, although I'm surprised to hear you say so," retorted her grandmother. "But in any case I'll be worried about you here on your own."

"I won't be on my own," Martine assured her. "Warrior and Shelby will keep me company and if I'm scared I can call Tendai. Besides, I've got some homework I need to finish."

At two o'clock she waved good-bye to her grandmother, smiling what she hoped was her most trustworthy smile. That in itself made Gwyn Thomas suspicious and before half an hour had gone by, Tendai was at the door, checking up on her. Luckily Martine, who really did have a school project to finish, was already sitting at the dining room table surrounded by books, so she had no difficulty convincing Tendai that she was absolutely fine. "I'll phone you in a second if I'm not," she promised.

Homework done, she went up to her room, shut the curtains on the afternoon sunshine, set the alarm, and hopped into bed. She had a long night ahead of her and she needed all the sleep she could get.

It was one a.m. when Martine entered the game reserve, nerves tingling, and she knew within seconds that there was going to be trouble. She crouched down in the thick grass and scanned the bush carefully. Lights were flickering in the trees. At this hour, that meant one of two things.

At best, it was Tendai or Alex patrolling the reserve, in which case if she was discovered and her grandmother heard about her escapade, her life would no longer be worth living. At worst, it was a gang of poachers—possibly even her grandfather's killers. Either way, it was a monumental disaster. Unable to get back without being seen, she used the grass as cover to make it as far as the trees and then flung herself under a clump of bushes.

Presently, she heard voices. The men were speaking softly, but it was a fine night and the sound traveled clearly over the water.

"I'm telling you, man, this better not be another one of your wild-goose chases," said one. "If we don't deliver this thing very soon, M . . ."—the name was lost on the wind—"is going to get ugly. He's not used to being kept waiting."

"When have I ever let you down?" a second voice demanded. "I'll find that blasted animal if it's the last thing I do."

The voices came nearer and one of the men stepped out of the trees. He walked to the water's edge and squatted to examine the mud with his flashlight.

"Bull's-eye!" he crowed.

Another man emerged from the shadows. Martine tried to get a good look at him, but despite the full moon, he was too far away to be anything other than an indistinct silhouette.

"What's up?"

"Giraffe tracks," the first man replied. He stood up. "Now all we have to do is find the giraffe."

There was a whisper of leaves and Martine whipped around in fright. It was Jemmy. Unheard, the giraffe had crept up almost beside her and now he loomed over her, outlined like a shimmering white giant against the blue-black sky. His eyes were locked on the two men.

"Jemmy!" Martine whispered. "You've got to go. Run! Get lost!"

He didn't move.

"Jemmy!" hissed Martine as loudly as she dared. "RUN!"

The white giraffe seemed to notice her for the first time. His liquid black eyes swept from her to the men and back again. He was shaking. Every inch of his body was poised for flight, but something was stopping him.

Abandoning all thought for her own safety, Martine jumped from her hiding place. "Go, Jemmy," she pleaded, drumming her fists against his leg. "You've got to go."

The white giraffe shoved her purposefully with his nose. That's when it hit Martine: He wanted her to come with him.

"There it is!" cried one of the men, and Martine went cold with terror. Behind her, she could hear shouts and the high-pitched whine of an engine firing into life. There was no escape. In a matter of minutes, she and Jemmy would be caught. Unless . . .

"Jemmy," yelled Martine, and she ran to the nearest climbable tree. For several petrifying moments it seemed as if Jemmy was not going to follow her, but all of a sudden he did. Martine pulled herself up onto the highest branch she could reach. There was no time to think. In particular, there was no time to think about how she'd never ridden any animal, not even a Shetland pony, and that she wasn't all that good at riding a bicycle. She simply swung onto Jemmy's back and grabbed a handful of mane.

The first panicked surge of the white giraffe nearly sent Martine flying. Self-preservation stopped her from falling off. Before she could adjust to the fact that she was ten feet off the ground—on the same level as a startled owl—they were bolting into the night. Martine leaned forward the way she'd seen horse riders do in England, gripped with her legs, and tried to avoid looking down.

They swept through the dark trees at an incredible speed, the giraffe galloping with a rhythmic, rocking-horse stride. How he avoided colliding with the overhead branches or getting a hoof caught in a root was a mystery to Martine. Nevertheless, once she got used to his sloping back, she found it surprisingly easy to ride him. He was broad and comfortable and his fur was like satin. Soon it seemed like the most natural thing in the world to be racing through the moonlight on the back of a young giraffe.

The sound of the men died behind them. After a while, Martine could hear nothing but the wind in her ears and the sharp cries of the night birds as they flashed by. Gradually, the trees gave way to open grassland and she could make out the shadows of the game reserve animals and smell the sweet smell of the bush at night. Zebras looked up blinking as they passed, a bush baby swung torch-like eyes on them, and a couple of lionesses bounded after them hungrily before stopping to lie in wait for easier prey.

After about a quarter of an hour they reached the lower slopes of the mountain that marked Sawubona's northern boundary and Jemmy slowed to a walk. His neck was wet with sweat and he was breathing hard, like a galloping racehorse. He seemed to be searching for something.

Martine was so exhilarated by the experience of riding a giraffe that at first she barely took in her surroundings. It was *awesome,* if a little vertigo-inducing, to see the world from this height. When she did look around, she found that they were in a barren clearing, littered with rocks and shale, at the base of a granite cliff. An air of desolation hung over the place. Usually the African night was alive with the sound of cicadas, frogs, and nocturnal creatures, but this area seemed devoid of any life. Even the temperature seemed lower. Nothing grew here apart from a single, twisted tree, which had taken root in the cliff itself and was shrouded in a tangled mass of moss and parasitic creepers. Due no doubt to the gales that ripped around the mountain, it had grown stunted and misshapen over the years and now, Martine thought with a shudder, it stood among the boulders like a sinister sentinel. She couldn't think why the white giraffe had brought her to this awful place, but he seemed very agitated. She began to feel concerned.

Through the night came the rumble of an engine. It was heading straight toward them. A searchlight swept the slopes above their heads.

"Jemmy!" Martine cried. "What are you *doing*? We've got to get away!"

Beneath her, she felt the white giraffe's hindquarters bunch as if he were preparing for a mighty leap. Martine put her arms around his neck and hung on for all she was worth. Until that moment, she'd been too full of the miracle of the ride to wonder where Jemmy was taking her or what would happen when they got there. Now reality was setting in. She dreaded to think how many bones she would break if she did crash to the ground, or indeed how she'd manage to crawl home and explain her injuries to her grandmother. Assuming, of course, that she wasn't eaten, bitten, stung, trampled, gored, or shot by poachers along the way. But there was no time to think about that now.

From standing, Jemmy took six breathtakingly fast strides and an enormous leap. In the instant before the jeep burst into the clearing and the world went black, Martine understood why Tendai had never been able to follow his tracks. The white giraffe had simply evaporated into thin air.

15

How they managed to survive this leap into the unknown, Martine later had no idea. One minute they were in the creepy clearing and the next Jemmy had launched himself directly at the cliff face, and Martine was being sucked at by gravity and strangled, mauled, and scratched by hairy vines and vicious thorny branches.

At last they came to a trembling halt. They were in complete darkness. It was some time before Martine's eyes adjusted to the light and she was able to take in the fact that she was still on the giraffe's back and still in one piece. It was even longer before she was able to figure out a way to slide safely to the ground.

Back on solid earth, she felt small and inconsequential again, but also elated. For the time being, at least, she and Jemmy had outwitted the poachers. She took her grandmother's flashlight from the pocket of her Windbreaker and prepared to expect the unexpected. She had willingly climbed onto the back of a wild giraffe (even though there were probably very good reasons why no one else in history had ever attempted to ride one) and had been whisked away to a deeply unpleasant place with an even more unpleasant tree. Then, just when she thought things couldn't possibly get any more surreal, the white giraffe had hurled himself at a mountain.

They could be anywhere.

She switched on her flashlight. Relief flooded through her. Nothing fantastical had occurred—at least nothing involving magic. And Jemmy hadn't actually jumped through bare rock. He'd simply leaped through the veil of creepers into the crevice that lay behind it. Because the crevice ran at an angle almost parallel to the cliff itself and was disguised by foliage and the great twisted bulk of the tree, it was invisible from the outside. Martine marveled that even the animals had ever found it. Not that many of them had, if the silence was anything to go by.

Drawing a wide arc with her flashlight beam, she discovered that she was in an exquisite little valley of perhaps an acre, surrounded on three sides by high sloping walls of sheer granite and on the fourth by massive chestnut boulders stacked five deep. The effect was of being on the inside of an uneven pyramid. The mountainside wall leaned at such an angle that it over-hung the boulders like a ledge, creating a roof over the valley. Seen from below, it was obvious that even if some-one were to climb the mountain and glance down, they still wouldn't notice the valley. It was completely hidden.

That wasn't the amazing part, though. Judging by the rectangle of blue-black sky she could see, a fluke of nature had ensured that there was enough space between the ledge and the boulders to allow sunlight into the valley for at least part of every day. That explained the presence of several acacia trees, a favorite food of the giraffe, the lush carpet of grass, and the fragrant white orchids springing from the valley's floor. There was also a pool of water in a hollowed rock, fed by a clear stream.

Martine knew she was standing in the white giraffe's secret sanctuary. Jemmy had everything he needed to survive here. Everything, that is, except love and company. No wonder he was so lonely. She ran a soothing hand over Jemmy and marveled once again that he stood still under her touch. If he would let her, she planned to give him all the love and company he could possibly want. He need never be lonely again.

In the meantime, a million questions ran through her mind. Who had first discovered the Secret Valley? Had any other human being ever been here? Did anyone apart from the animals know it existed?

She set out to explore the valley perimeter, combing the walls with her flashlight. That's when she saw it—a black triangle between two rocks. It looked like some sort of tunnel. Immediately she felt an overwhelming urge to investigate. She was well aware that there were probably smarter things she could do in her present situation than go poking around in black holes, but try as she might, she couldn't think of any. She checked on the white giraffe. He was over by the stream drinking deeply, his front legs spread wide, his silvery nose wrinkled against the bubbles.

Martine debated what to do. What if she'd used up all her luck for one evening? But there was something almost magnetic about the space. She felt as if it were pulling her toward it—*calling* her, even. She had the oddest sense that going into the tunnel was what she was meant to do. That that's what she'd end up doing whether she decided to or not.

Retying her boot laces purposefully, Martine walked on uncertain legs toward the black hole. Her heart was in her mouth.

It was a tunnel, one that smelled strongly of wet rock and animals that dwell in dank, dark places—spiders, baboons, and the like. Leopards enjoy those places as well, but Martine consoled herself with the thought that Jemmy would hardly have lived as long as he had if a carnivore resided so close by. After one last attempt to talk herself into staying in the lovely valley, she stepped inside.

The tunnel was not much taller than she was, and even

a small adult would have had to crouch, but gradually it widened and became less claustrophobic. After a while, it turned back on itself. She was beneath the mountain now. From there, the ground rose sharply in a series of steep steps, slick with froggy algae. Martine put the flashlight between her teeth and scrambled up in an undignified fashion. She made a mental note to smuggle her giraffe-fur, grass, and slime-covered jeans into the washing machine before her grandmother noticed them. The vegetable garden excuse was not going to work a second time.

She was halfway up the last step when a hideous screech echoed from the chamber above her. Martine nearly flew over backward. Her light flashed around madly as she grabbed a ledge to save herself. Within seconds, the air was filled with a blizzard of flapping wings and high-pitched squeaks. She had unleashed a colony of bats!

In England, Martine had known girls who went around saying that they had a phobia about bats, even though they lived in suburbia and had never encountered them outside Dracula films. She herself had never much cared for the idea of them. But since her arrival in Africa she'd come to realize that they were actually quite cute. Far from being blood-sucking vampires, they were just flying mice that enjoyed fruit. Until, that is, they got caught in your hair.

"Ugh," spluttered Martine as she tried to disentangle their scratchy feet and clammy wings without being bitten. "Ugh!"

106

When the black whirlwind subsided, she picked up her flashlight, dusted herself off, and saw that she was in a cave—one the height and size of a small church. But what struck her as strange was that the feeling in the cave was different from that of the tunnel, which was simply damp and cold. The cave had a distinct atmosphere. Martine took a lungful of its dense, heavy air and was immediately swamped with the same light-headed, time-travel sensation that she'd felt in some of the cathedrals and historic buildings her parents had taken her to in England—Leeds Castle or the Tower of London. There, too, she'd had a real sense of the generations who'd occupied them before. It was almost as if certain people in certain eras made their mark on a place so thoroughly that their spirit never left. But why should she feel that here?

Moving cautiously so as not to alarm the bats, Martine shined her flashlight around the cave. What she saw next made her cry out in wonder. Every wall and every rock was covered in paintings! Some of them were nothing more than crude charcoal line drawings, faded with the years. Some were stick figures. And some were so rich in texture and hue that they seemed to leap from the walls like naked flames. But every one of them lived and breathed. They spoke to her from across the ages as clearly as if their creators were standing in front of her, telling her of battles lost and won, feasts and famines, times of pestilence and times of plenty.

Martine sank down onto a rock. Half of her felt like

a child at Christmas; the other half felt dizzy. What was happening? What was this all about? Jemmy, the kudu, and now the cave pictures . . . ? What did it all mean? Oh, if only she'd been able to have a proper conversation with Grace on that first day in Africa. Martine was sure that Grace held the key to at least some part of the mystery. She had, after all, known about the gift.

So much was happening so fast. Martine tried to remember her life with her mum and dad. Already bits of it were fading. One thing she did recall was being petrified of the dark and spending sleepless nights convinced that something monstrous lurked under her bed. Several times she'd even crept into her parents' room. Yet here she was, alone in a cave in the dead of night, and she felt completely unafraid. Confused, yes, but not afraid. Nor did she feel alone. It was as though her mum and dad were watching her, as though they knew about her and Jemmy. She smiled to herself in the dark.

She knew that she owed much of her newfound confidence to the white giraffe. Loving Jemmy had given her a reason to smile when she was sure that she'd never smile again, and being brave for Jemmy, as she'd had to tonight, had made her reach deep inside for some strong, steady part of herself that she hadn't even known existed until then. In return, the white giraffe had overcome his fear of humans to save her twice and allow her to ride him. If he hadn't trusted her, he wouldn't have brought her here. She vowed that as long as she lived she would never tell anyone about the Secret Valley. If the paintings were ever found, Jemmy's sanctuary would be flooded with reporters, scientists, and tourists. The ancient spirits would be chased away. The world would come trampling in.

Martine stared at the paintings. One of her mum's books had contained pictures just like these. They'd been painted by the San people, as the Bushmen were known, centuries before the white man ever came, using iron ore, china clay, and oxgall. She wondered if these pictures, too, had been painted by the Bushmen, or if some other tribe had done them—perhaps Tendai's tribe, the Zulus. She got up off the rock and went over for a closer look. Her head was still spinning and she still had millions of questions, but mostly she just felt lucky to be able to witness this.

Holding the flashlight above her head, she walked around the cave. The red, gold, and black images unfolded before her, like scenes from an old sepia-toned movie. Martine was entranced. Despite their simplicity, they conveyed lives of great beauty and sorrow. There were fantastic scenes of animal migration, tribal dances, and men confronting rhinos and elephants armed only with bows and arrows. She was halfway around when she noticed a painting of a giraffe. It was one of a series, most of which featured herds of giraffes surrounded by men with spears. In each new picture, the herds became smaller and smaller, and more and more bloody giraffes lay on the ground. Soon there were just two left. Then they, too, were on the ground and a man lay on the ground with them. But it was when she saw the next painting that Martine's head really started whirling. It showed a white giraffe suckling from an elephant. At first, she was sure that the coloring of the giraffe was merely a trick of the light, but when she compared it to the previous images, it was definitely paler. She traced the giraffe with her fingertips. The rock was cold to the touch but somehow it, too, had a kind of energy.

She had to force herself to look at the final picture and when she did, the emotion was overwhelming. The hue of the image was different, almost as if it had been created with a metallic paint. In it, a child was riding a white giraffe. To the left of them was a fire and to the right was a line of animals of different species.

"The child who can ride a white giraffe will have power over all the animals," Tendai had told her when she arrived. And although some dreamy part of her had entertained fantasies about riding Jemmy, she'd never really thought about what it meant because she had never believed for a second it might come true. Why would she imagine she'd be able to ride a giraffe? Nobody else in the world ever had.

The child who can ride a white giraffe will have power over all the animals.

For the second time that evening, Martine's knees gave way and she had to sit down on another rock.

Grace had been right. The forefathers had known she was coming.

16

In the excitement of the night, Martine had forgotten about the poachers and the fact that she was miles from home with dawn rapidly approaching. Even supposing she was able to steer Jemmy—who was not, after all, a schooled horse—in the general direction of the house, there was no way she could allow him to leave the Secret Valley if there was any possibility that the hunters were still out looking for him.

After a last bemused glance at the giraffe paintings, Martine ran to the cave exit and slipped and slithered back down the rocky steps, adding a fresh layer of moss to her jeans. The tunnel seemed longer than she remembered and she was very grateful to reach the tranquil valley and hear the welcoming call of the white giraffe. She rushed over to Jemmy, put her face against his velvet fur, and cuddled him for several minutes. Only then did she switch off her flashlight and grope her way to the valley entrance. Standing on a rock, she peered over the edge of the crevice. The dense foliage of the tree blanketed out most but not all of the view. A stamp-sized gap showed a patch of sky, which was that brilliant blue that precedes first light. Martine could also make out the front half of the poachers' rusting Ford pickup. It was empty.

Seeing the truck gave her an idea. Like a lot of her ideas recently, it was a bit crazy, but if it worked, it would be the perfect solution. She was going to get the poachers to give her a ride home!

Martine ran through the dark valley to Jemmy's side. She stood on tiptoes and he put his head down and nuzzled her affectionately. "Stay safe, my beautiful friend," she said. A little self-consciously, she added, "I love you."

She returned to the valley entrance, climbed cautiously over the sharp rocks that guarded it, and began to wriggle through the tangle of sticky creepers. Lying on her belly beneath the sinister tree, she waited and listened. Twin points of light were bobbing through the trees. The poachers were returning to their vehicle!

For a second Martine's limbs were filled with the same helpless weakness she'd felt on the night of the fire, but she propelled herself forward. If she hesitated now, it was over. Tearing herself free of the vines, she sprinted for the truck and flung herself on the back. A tarpaulin lay in a heap near the cab. Martine dived under it, gagging at its rotten-meat odor. Then she lay still. She hardly dared breathe.

Footsteps crunched across the stony ground. The truck rocked as the men got in and the doors slammed with unnecessary force. They weren't speaking. Despite her predicament, Martine managed a smile. She pictured them seething, each blaming the other for a wasted, torturous night among the creepies and crawlies. With any luck, it had put them off hunting for life.

The old truck gave a harsh metal wheeze and jolted into action. Martine's plan was to wait until the poachers slowed down to open a gate or cut the fence and then jump out. Assuming that she didn't injure herself in the fall, she should then be within easy walking distance of the house.

In the meantime, she was determined to try to get a good look at the men. Using the tarp as a cover, she raised herself up inch by inch until her eyes were level with the bottom of the dusty cab window. The first pink stirrings of dawn were in the sky and Martine saw immediately why she'd found it so difficult to make out the features of the men at the waterhole. They were dressed in gray long-sleeved shirts, and black ski masks covered their faces. All she could see was their hands—the driver's powerful paws gripping the wheel, and his accomplice's hairy ones holding his rifle.

She lay back down again. One of the men was black, with a tattoo of a tiger on his wrist, and one was white. It didn't really tell her anything. It didn't even tell her if they were the same men who had shot her grandfather and the two giraffes.

A lightbulb went on in her head. *What if the clue lay not with the men but with the giraffe?*

From what Tendai said, the police and everyone at Sawubona had always assumed that the poachers had been after ordinary giraffes, mainly because it was ordinary giraffes that had been found dead, and most people believed that the white giraffe was only a legend. But what if they had been trying to catch the white giraffe instead? That would change everything.

Martine wriggled deeper into the folds of the stinking tarpaulin. It made total sense. For the poachers to have known of the white giraffe's existence, they must have had very close links with Sawubona. That meant they were either friends or relatives of someone who worked on the game reserve, or they worked at Sawubona themselves. Martine shivered at the thought of these possibilities. She knew that Alex had befriended her grandfather in the year before he died and had been promised the job of game warden if anything ever happened to him. Alex had also threatened Martine herself, had shot the kudu and found it amusing, and had made it clear that he knew the value of the white giraffe and was very sure it existed.

But maybe he was too obvious a suspect. In Martine's mum's favorite detective show, the villain had never turned out to be the weird postal worker with the limp or the gun enthusiast or the eccentric, wart-ridden spinster. It was always the least obvious person—the clean-cut doctor, the wholesome housewife, or the new vicar.

The least obvious person at Sawubona was—and Martine felt guilty for even thinking such a thing—Tendai. He claimed he'd been away in the north of the country at the time of the shooting, visiting his relatives. But what if he hadn't been away at all? What if he'd been right here? What if the reason he didn't find the poachers' tracks was because he didn't want to?

But no, that didn't work either, because Martine *refused* to believe it was true. She would trust Tendai with her life.

The vehicle slowed. Martine readied herself for the jump. She dreaded to think what would happen if the driver or his gun-toting companion noticed her reflection in the mirror.

In the end it was easier than she expected, largely because the poachers swerved to avoid a startled springbok and Martine flew over the side. She landed in a clump of dewy, elephant-dung-padded grass, which had the double effect of cushioning her fall and quickly obscuring her from view. It did not, however, improve the fragrance of her jeans. By the time she had established that her left leg was bruised rather than broken, all that remained of the poachers was the fading drone of their engine. She checked around her for animals in search of breakfast. She was not, as she'd hoped, close to the house, but she could see the faint outline of the Sawubona sign and knew that she was close to the road.

With dawn unfurling like a scarlet banner above her head and the birds competing to announce the arrival of another perfect summer's day, Martine managed a limping jog through the bush to the game gate and was home in under ten minutes. Usually her heart would have been full of the magnificence of the morning and the fizzing freshness of the air, but today all she could think about was the danger Jemmy was in and how close they'd both come to falling victim to the hunters.

A couple of hours later Martine had showered and put on her uniform, and she was in the process of shoving her jeans to the very back of the washing machine and thinking how nice it was to have the house to herself, when she heard what sounded like a stock car race in the yard. She rushed outside expecting to see her grandmother returning from Somerset West and was confronted instead with an extraordinary sight. Police were spilling out of two squad cars. But that wasn't what stopped her in her tracks. In the center of the lawn, roped together like the bad guys in a cowboy film, were the poachers. Their ski masks were gone and their faces were as sour as milk, but there was no mistaking them.

Tendai, Alex, and her grandmother were in a huddle in the driveway, talking intently, but they broke apart when Martine walked up.

"Martine, thank goodness you're okay," said Gwyn

Thomas, rushing forward. Her overnight bag and car keys were still on the lawn where she'd dropped them. "I've just arrived home to find police swarming all over Sawubona. Alex here has managed, almost single-handedly, to catch the poachers who have been plaguing us for nearly two years."

"Alex?" Martine burst out before she could stop herself.

Her grandmother gave her a reproachful look. "Yes, Alex," she said. "In an act of extraordinary bravery, he shot out the poachers' front tires as they left the game reserve. Then he radioed for help and managed to pin one of the men to the ground until Tendai could get there and assist him to catch the other."

"It was nothing, ma'am," said the game warden. "That's what you hired me for. I just wish I could have done it sooner." He put his arm around the Zulu's shoulders and said warmly, "But I couldn't have done it at all without Tendai's help."

Martine caught Tendai's eye, but he looked away quickly.

Her grandmother glanced at her watch. "We'd better get you to school, Martine," she said. "If you collect your things, I'll take you in myself."

Martine, who in the space of ten hours had ridden a white giraffe, escaped from men with guns, and seen her destiny written on a cave wall, was struggling to cope with this unexpected turn of events, but she went crossly back to the house to collect her lunch box and backpack.

Alex, the hero! How sickening. How maddening. Was it really possible that she'd been mistaken about that strawberry-blond troll?

She was on the kitchen step when footsteps pounded up behind her. "Martine," called Alex. "Wait up."

Martine turned with a scowl, but the arrogance that usually marred Alex's face had been replaced by a puppy-ish eagerness.

"Martine," he said, "I owe you a huge apology. Over the past year I've become so obsessed with catching the people who were stealing your grandmother's animals that at times it's clouded my judgment. I don't know what came over me the day I drove you to school. Threatening you like that—it was unforgivable. But I was worried that a stranger to Sawubona, someone not familiar with the wildlife, might get in the way of my investigation. All I can say is I'm sorry. If there's anything I can do to make it up to you, let me know." He reached into his pocket and brought out an exquisite kingfisher feather. "Peace offering?" he asked.

Martine accepted it grudgingly but didn't answer. She was remembering the bullet splitting the tree above Tendai's head and the haunting eyes of the fallen kudu.

Alex's mouth gave a twist. "Yeah, I know what you're thinking. The kudu: Why did I shoot it? Believe me, it hurt me to do it. But I'd become suspicious of everyone by then and it was a test. I wanted to see how Tendai would react. And he reacted the way a man who cares about animals *should* react. So he was in the clear. But you never know in this game. When there's a lot of money at stake, even the best can be tempted."

Martine wasn't convinced, but then she didn't *not* believe him either. She decided that the best way forward was to trust nobody and say nothing. After the night's adventures, one thing was perfectly clear: She and Jemmy were on their own.

17

It was late summer in South Africa. More than a month had gone by since Martine had first met Jemmy and in that time her life had changed beyond imagining. Not that it had all been easy. After her flight from the Secret Valley, nine agonizing days had passed before she caught so much as a glimpse of the white giraffe, and then it had been so dark and the vision of him so fleeting that she *sensed* he was there rather than saw him. Naturally, her grandmother had chosen that very evening to embark on an all-night session with the game reserve accounts and there was absolutely no chance of Martine sneaking out undetected. She just had to sit in her room and fume.

By the tenth day she was ready to tear her hair out. It didn't help that ever since the incident at the Botanical Gardens, the Five Star Gang had tormented her. They put chocolate on her chair so that when she stood up she had a brown sticky mess all over her uniform. It happened at nine a.m., which meant Martine had to spend the rest of the day being snickered at by the whole school. She found *umthakathi* and *witch* scrawled all over her books, and on another occasion she opened her pencil case to find a hairy baboon spider—an African tarantula—lurking inside. Martine screamed so loudly that Miss Volkner immediately banned her from speaking for the rest of the day.

Not that that was very difficult. After what had happened at Kirstenbosch, few children talked to Martine anyway. The Five Star Gang had turned them against her. And Ben, to whom she would have liked to speak, remained a mystery. When he passed her on the way to class, his mouth curled up at the edges as if he was happy to see her, but he never spoke. Even after he rescued her, he hadn't said a word. And at recess he no longer sat under the far tree in the playing fields but took himself away to some unknown location.

All these things conspired to make Martine feel tearful and lonely again, even though she was getting along much better with her grandmother. With the white giraffe gone, the emptiness she'd felt after losing her mum and dad returned. What if Jemmy was caught in a snare? What if he, too, was gone forever? Oh, why hadn't she spent any time trying to teach him some sort of signal so that she could call him?

She scoured the books in her bedroom and in the school library for more information on giraffes, hoping to learn something that might help her, but the only new fact she came across was that the Romans had called the giraffe *camelopardalis,* meaning "camel marked like a leopard," which was interesting but of no use at all.

Then, out of the blue, she had a brainstorm. It happened when she came across a book on dogs on her bookshelf. In his youth, her grandfather had apparently been a very fine dog trainer and there was a jade box on top of the cabinet in the living room containing three of his old dog whistles. In a rare moment of sharing, her grandmother had told her that one of the whistles was completely silent to the human ear because it was pitched at a frequency that only dogs could hear.

But what if giraffes could hear it too?

That night, Martine crept out to the garden and experimented with the silent whistle. For nearly an hour she blew and blew, but nothing happened. Martine stood shivering and frustrated under the mango trees, convinced that she'd never see Jemmy again. Then, a miracle. The white giraffe came striding out of the darkness and stood beside the skeleton tree. Martine did a double take. She'd imagined seeing him again so many times that she wondered for a second if she'd conjured him up. But he was real. Not only that, he was looking right at her, just as he had done on the night of the storm.

Martine didn't even pause to check for lions or leopards. She just went tearing through the game park gate and running and stumbling along the water hole track, sending all manner of night creatures fleeing for their lives. When she reached the giraffe he lowered his head and she flung her arms around his neck with such enthusiasm that he snorted with alarm and backed off a little, even though he was obviously just as pleased to see her. "Jemmy," said Martine, "thank you for coming back to me."

In her fantasies, she'd always followed this moment by hopping on the white giraffe's back and being whisked away to the Secret Valley, but in real life Jemmy was an untamed animal as tall as your average tree, and Martine knew as much about training wildlife as she did about riding a unicycle on a high wire at a circus, so there were one or two practicalities to overcome.

She found, for instance, that there really was such a thing as beginner's luck. The first time she rode Jemmy he stood quietly beside a tree and allowed her to climb onto his back, but this concept seemed to have vanished from his mind entirely. Now when she attempted it, Jemmy waited until she was suspended between the tree and his back before spying some juicy acacia leaves and moving away. Martine had to improvise a sort of flying dive and latch on to his neck. There she dangled until her arms nearly came out of their sockets. At that point, she tumbled the very long way to the ground.

Jemmy didn't understand what he'd done, but he made his low, musical fluttering sound and nuzzled her with his silver nose until Martine forgot about the pain in her backside and remembered how much she adored him. I have to be patient, she told herself. She also tried to put herself in his position. If she were a giraffe and someone rubbed the back of her forelegs and tugged gently on her knees, she figured that eventually she'd understand that they wanted her to lie down. So she experimented with Jemmy and, after some trial and error, he did. And before the night was over, Martine was flying through the moonlight again on the back of a young giraffe.

That was only the start of it, though, because she then had to learn to steer Jemmy and stop him. It didn't happen overnight and there were several close calls over the next few weeks while they got to know each other—once the giraffe shied away from a bristling porcupine and Martine was nearly impaled on its black and white spines—but through it all Jemmy was gentle and loving and when he did grasp what she was trying to teach him, he grasped it completely, and it was as if he'd always known it.

For Martine, it was then that the door opened on the *real* Africa, the hidden Africa; the Africa that few human beings apart from the Bushmen ever witnessed. Those nights with Jemmy were the most magical of Martine's life. It was rare for the other animals to notice her, and those that did seemed to accept her as an extension of the white giraffe. Safe on Jemmy's high back, she was able to watch baby warthogs play and move close enough to elephants to touch their parched, grooved skin. Once, when Jemmy was drinking from a lake as black as ink, she found herself just yards from a party of bubble-blowing hippos. With their tubby bodies, piggy eyes, and tiny ears, hippos were among the cutest creatures in the wild, but they were also among the most lethal. Their huge pink jaws could bite boats as well as people in half—and frequently did—so Martine took special care to stay still and respectful whenever she was anywhere near them.

But her favorite thing was to ride the white giraffe up the escarpment where she and Tendai had had breakfast, swivel around so she could use his withers as a pillow and his hindquarters as a footrest, lie back, and gaze at the canopy of stars. So clear and cold were the nights, with summer sliding into autumn, that she was able to see the Southern Cross and Orion's Belt and even Mars, glowing red in the navy blue sky.

Sometimes she talked to Jemmy about what had happened to her. About the night of the fire and how scared and heartbroken she'd been. About her mum and dad and how much she missed them. About school and her struggles to fit in. About the Egyptian goose and the kudu, and the strangeness of her gift. Jemmy's ears flicked back and forth and he made his musical fluttering sound, and somehow she felt that in his giraffe way he understood everything and she felt comforted.

The whistle, it turned out, worked perfectly. Jemmy always responded to it if he could hear it, although how long it took depended on where he was in the reserve. Martine took to wearing the whistle around her neck, even at school, because it made her feel close to Jemmy. It also meant that she didn't have to hunt for it when she went sneaking out to see him late at night. But as much as she missed him, she was very careful to vary the hours when she called him and never to do it more than twice a week. She was well aware that each time she went into the reserve she was taking a risk.

Still she continued to get away with it and she managed to persuade herself—mainly because she wanted more than anything for it to be true—that she and Jemmy could go on like this forever.

18

A part from her mum and dad, the person Martine thought more about than any other on those star-flung nights was Grace. It was Grace, she was convinced, who held the key to the questions she had about her gift. She hadn't forgotten the African woman's wonderful food, nor how warm Grace was to her on that traumatic first day and how determined she'd been that Martine should know the truth about the secrets at Sawubona. Yet Martine hadn't seen her since. Once or twice she'd considered skipping school to try to find her, but she wasn't sure where Grace lived and Tendai refused to be part of it.

"Your grandmother would not like it," was his last word on the subject.

Later that same evening—at half past midnight, to be precise—Martine thought how much less Gwyn Thomas would like it if she could see her granddaughter crouched low over the neck of a white giraffe as he galloped at full speed for the black mountain that marked Sawubona's boundary. She was going in search of answers. If Tendai and her grandmother weren't going to tell her anything about the past, and if she was banned from seeing Grace, who possibly could, then she would find the information for herself in the only place she could think of to look: the Secret Valley.

It was a balmy night. The wind in her face was pungent with the smell of the bush, and the moon was a bold yellow sliver. As she rode, she remembered a wonderful Bushman legend she heard from Samson, the old man who cared for the animals in Sawubona's orphanage. In the story, the moon was a man who had angered the sun. Every month, when the moon was full, the jealous sun would take his knife and cut away a piece of him until only a thin slice remained. The moon would plead for that piece to be left for his children. His wish granted, he would build himself up again until he was once more prosperous and whole.

Martine snapped into the present to find they'd reached the barren clearing. The twisted tree glared at them, guarding its secret like a living beast. Martine tried not to look at it. Knotting her fingers through Jemmy's mane, she urged him forward. Vines and branches tore at her skin as he jumped. It was like being ripped from his back by an octopus. Then, just as suddenly as before, it was still and dark. She was in the Secret Valley. All she could hear was the tinkling of the stream and the giraffe's rapid breathing. The scent of orchids wafted up to her. Above her head, the gap in the valley roof showed a rectangle of blue-black sky sprinkled with stars.

She slid down Jemmy's neck and switched on her flashlight. The tunnel entrance was in front of her, as spookily inviting as before. A prickle of fear brushed her skin. What if something went wrong? Nobody knew where she was. Nobody even knew about the Secret Valley. In the unlikely event anyone ever found her, all they'd stumble across would be her bones, just like the slave at Skeleton Stream. But she banished these thoughts from her head. She had an hour at most to look for the truth. She needed to start down the tunnel.

Martine stood in the center of the cave, bathed in the radiant glow of the paintings. She filled her lungs with its dense, cathedral air. The time-travel sensation she'd felt before, the vivid sense of generations past, was stronger than ever. There was something humbling about it. It made her feel as tiny as an ant or a fleck of dust in a gale—at the mercy of some immense, unseen power. She went over to the painting of the white giraffe and its child rider and traced its shining outline with her fingertips.

"I see you found the message from the forefathers, chile."

Martine tried to yelp, but her throat sealed up with shock and she just gulped like a haddock out of water.

Grace stepped out of the shadows. She was draped from head to foot in Zulu tribal dress. Beaded jewelry in all the colors of the rainbow adorned her arms and throat.

"Grace!" croaked Martine. "What are you doing here? How did you get here? Who else knows about this place? Does Tendai?"

"So many questions," said Grace. She smiled, but even in the wavering light Martine could see that the smile didn't reach her eyes. She seemed burdened somehow, weighted down with worry. "Come," she said. "Come sit with old Grace."

Martine followed her to the corner of the cave, where the water-hewn rocks made a natural bench. They sat side by side, gazing at the gallery of copper and ochre paintings. Martine was still reeling from the bombshell of finding the woman she'd wanted so much to see, here, in this sacred place.

"What you got to understand, chile, is that this arl started a long time ago, before my grandmamma was born and her grandmamma before her, when Bushmen lived on the land you now call Sawubona. Everything that will come is already written. Even the white giraffe. You see for yourself your story on this here wall."

She raised her arm and Martine saw for the first time that there was an order to the pictures; their tales of beauty and tragedy unfolded like the plot of a novel.

"Grace," Martine asked in a hushed tone, "what happened to the people who stayed in this cave?"

"They perished, chile, arl but one—a girl. The elders of our tribe say that it was a disease brought by the white man—chicken pox or some'at, but nobody know for sure. As the end drew near for each of 'em, they painted their stories and the legends of the forefathers on these walls. Then there was just one. She was found by one of my grannies from long, long ago—she was a *sangoma*, a traditional healer, like me—in the place outside the valley. My mama say that on that day the *sangoma* call down so many favors from the gods that fire rained from the heavens and scorched the earth so bad that nothin' could ever grow there no more."

Martine thought about the barren clearing and the glowering tree, misshapen and parasitic, and had no trouble believing the tale.

"After the Bushman girl was well," Grace went on, "she brought the *sangoma* here, to the Memory Room. She made har promise that only har firstborn daughter and har firstborn daughter after har—all *sangomas*—should know the secrets of the caves. And you, chile, the chile who rides the white giraffe."

Martine stared around the cave with new eyes. "But why me? What does it have to do with me?"

"The answers are right here on the walls," Grace said again, "but only time and experience will give you eyes to see them."

Martine looked harder than ever at the paintings, hoping that, in spite of Grace's words, she'd find the answers now, when she felt she most needed them. But their fiery colors just blurred before her vision and only one image stayed clear: the child on the white giraffe.

"Grace," she said, "does Tendai know about the white giraffe?"

"He ain't sure," replied Grace. "Tendai, he still a young man and young people are always suspicious of the old ways. They call it mumbo jumbo. *Supastishun.*" She studied Martine with strange glittering eyes. "But not you, huh?"

"No," said Martine, "not me."

It was on the tip of Martine's tongue to ask Grace how she'd known she would find her in the cave on this particular night and at this particular time, but she decided against it. Some things were better left unsaid.

Instead she asked, "Grace, why did you come here tonight?"

Again Martine thought she saw a shadow pass over the African woman's face. "I come with a warnin'," Grace said heavily. "Your time is almost here. Dark forces be comin' and they will stop at nothin' to get to the white giraffe. Be very careful. Trust in your gift and it will keep you safe."

Martine had a sudden premonition of danger. She'd convinced herself that, with the poachers caught, no one would bother Jemmy ever again. But even as Grace spoke, she knew the woman's words were true. The hunters would be back.

"I don't care what happens to me, but how can I save the white giraffe?" she pleaded.

In answer, Grace opened the beaded pouch that hung from her neck. She took out a handful of small corked bottles that sparkled in the light. Their contents were orange, brown, mustard yellow, and a peculiarly vile green. She smiled, and this time her eyes did light up and crinkle at the corners.

"Grace is gonna teach you," she said.

For the next hour, Martine—who knew that she should be getting back but was too entranced to care—had a crash course in Zulu traditional medicine. She learned about plants like mother-in-law's tongue, which is a remedy for pain and earaches, rooibos tea, which can cure stomach cramps and allergies, and many other healing herbs besides. Afterward, Grace handed the pouch full of bottles to Martine.

"Thank you, Grace," she said. "I'll keep them in a special place."

Grace looked pleased. "You're mos' welcome. You have your healing gift, but sometimes you will need a little extra help."

There were so many questions and no more time to ask them, but there was one thing Martine had to know before they parted.

"Grace," she said, "why doesn't my grandmother want me here?"

"She do want you here, chile. She do. Your granny loves you *soooo* much. But she has her story just like you have yours."

Martine was about to tell Grace that her grandmother had no feelings for her whatsoever when Grace cut in. "Now *I* want to ax you somethin'. I got a cousin of mine who works down at your school and he tells me that you're arl the time arl by yourself. Why you don't find yourself some friends to play with? It ain't good to be alone."

Martine dropped her eyes, embarrassed. "But I have got a friend. The white giraffe is my friend."

"That's right, the giraffe is your friend. But every chile needs someone their own age, a human bei', to talk with. To *share* with."

"Well, maybe there's no one I want to be friends with," Martine said defensively. "Who would understand about Jemmy? Who would understand about this?"

For a long time Grace made no comment. Finally she laid a hand on Martine's shoulder. "You will find the friend you seek in the last place you look."

19

Three days later Martine was walking across the playing fields after a soccer game, her head still full of her encounter with Grace, when she heard raised voices coming from Black Horse Ravine. Her first thought was that someone was in trouble. Black Horse Ravine was a deep gorge with a fast-flowing river, which lay beyond the boundary fence of the school. It was so treacherous that the punishment for even entering the dark pines that fronted it was ten detentions. But Martine didn't hesitate. She climbed over the fence and ran into the trees. When she was out of sight of any passing teacher, she squatted down and listened.

Right away, she recognized the voices of the Five Star Gang. They seemed to be taunting somebody. "You think you're pretty clever, don't you? Did you really think you could make fools of us and get away with it?"

"Tell us the truth or you're going for a swim. It was your twisted little brain that came up with the plan to humiliate us at the Botanical Gardens, wasn't it? Answer us. And don't pretend you can't speak. The teachers might be taken in by your act, but we are not."

There was no response from their captive.

"He's such a waste of space, isn't he?" Scott said. "I mean, look at him. You're a runt, Buddha, you know that. I've seen chickens with more meat on their bones."

"You're a loony, has anyone ever told you that? You're a freak."

"You're like one of those sad-looking dogs you find down at the shelter," jeered Luke. "Say: 'I'm a mongrel, Luke.' What are you? Say: 'I'm a mongrel . . .'"

Martine had until then been crouching behind a boulder, too scared to intervene. But at those words, the memory of Tendai's story came burning through her like liquid fire. With a yell of fury, she burst out of the trees. Luke and Scott had hold of Ben and were forcing him to stand on the edge of the ravine. Lucy was laughing her high-pitched laugh and Pieter was sitting on the ground nearby looking slightly green.

"What are you?" Luke was saying to Ben.

He didn't see Martine until she was right in front of him and then he just stammered, "M-Martine! What the . . . ?"

"I'll tell you who Ben is," Martine heard herself saying.

"He's my friend, that's who he is. He's also the boy who beat you by about fifty meters in the hundred meters at the school championships, Luke. And he's the boy whose homework you keep borrowing, Lucy, because you're too thick to do your own. As for his parents, well, at least he's got a father, Scott. When was the last time you saw yours?"

A shocked silence followed her outburst. The Black Horse River roared far below them.

"My f-father . . ." stammered Scott. "Oh, forget it. This is no fun. Come on, Luke, Lucy, Pieter. Let's leave these losers to their pathetic little friendship."

He dropped Ben's arm so abruptly that the boy teetered for a moment on the edge of the ravine before finding his balance and stepping away.

They left noisily, kicking at pine cones, cursing as they went. Martine and Ben were alone.

Martine suddenly felt shy. "Are you okay?" she asked hesitantly.

It struck her for the first time that Ben was very handsome. He had topaz eyes like a lion, shiny black hair, and white, even teeth. When he spoke, his voice was soft and he pronounced each word clearly and separately, like a newscaster.

"I appreciate your help," he said, "but I prefer to fight my own battles."

For several days after the incident at Black Horse Ravine, Martine went back to feeling nervous again at school. She was convinced that the Five Star Gang would want to get back at her somehow. Instead, something completely different happened. By standing up to them, she seemed to have earned their respect. Lucy van Heerden presented her with a box of homemade condensed-milk cookies to apologize and all five of them went out of their way to be nice to her.

Martine was cool with them at first—she was still angry about the way they'd treated Ben at the ravine and the wild goose at the Botanical Gardens. But they kept telling her that both were just games that had gone too far and that they felt really bad about them, and gradually she came to believe they'd changed. That didn't mean that Martine wanted to be bosom buddies with them, but it did mean that when their close friend Sherilyn offered her a slice of carrot cake and wanted to sit with her, she accepted, and when Xhosa asked her about life on Sawubona, she was happy to go along with that too. She kept remembering Grace's words: *You will find the friend you seek in the last place you look.* Maybe Grace had been right about that too.

Of course, Ben was still Ben and he still spent all his free time by himself. Ever since Martine had intervened at Black Horse Ravine he seemed to have gone out of his way to avoid her. Lucy had given him a box of apology cookies too, but he'd later been seen handing them out to some homeless children. At recess, he once again sat cross-legged under the distant trees with his palms resting on his knees and turned upward. Some days Martine was convinced that he was meditating.

Now that she knew he wasn't mute—that he actually had a beautiful speaking voice and was, as she'd thought all along, very smart—she spent a lot of time puzzling over why he never talked to anyone at school. Finally she'd come to the conclusion that he just couldn't be bothered. Maybe school and the people in it didn't interest him. Maybe he was only here because he had to be. Maybe he was happiest when he was in nature, like Tendai. But just when Martine had made up her mind to get to the bottom of the riddle that was Ben once and for all, two things came along to preoccupy her. She began to get the distinct impression someone was going through her locker. Nothing was ever taken and the changes, if there were any, were subtle ones—workbooks curled up at the corners as if they'd been flicked through, items shifted or replaced in a different order—but it was still creepy. Then a tiny watercolor she'd done of Jemmy went missing. She spent so long searching for it that she was late for her next lesson.

"Ah, Martine," said Miss Volkner when Martine burst in. "Good of you to join us."

Martine was mumbling an apology when the teacher interrupted, "We were just discussing African folklore. Lucy asked a question about giraffes."

"Giraffes!" cried Martine.

"Yes, those creatures with the funny long necks," said

Miss Volkner, who was irritated with Martine for being late. "Do you have a problem with that? I'd have thought you'd be the class expert, living on a game reserve."

Martine was about to deny that she knew anything at all about giraffes when something stopped her. It wasn't often that she got a chance to talk about her favorite subject. Besides, she thought mischievously, she could have a bit of fun with it.

"No," she said. "I mean, no, I don't have a problem with it."

"Good, then perhaps you can tell us what you know."

So Martine, flushing a little with shyness, told the class how the ancients had regarded giraffes as the most innocent, delicate, and timid of all the wild animals, but also brave enough to fight dragons. How the Venda people called them *thutlwa*, "rising above the trees," and how other tribes saw a giraffe in the stars: the Southern Cross. She also told them some facts. That giraffes can reach speeds of thirty-five miles per hour and that it takes them ten years to reach their full height of seventeen feet for females and nineteen feet for males.

Miss Volkner was clearly taken aback. "If you applied yourself to your school subjects with even half the diligence with which you appear to study wildlife, your grades would improve dramatically," she said somewhat sarcastically.

"Miss Volkner," asked Sherilyn, "has anyone ever ridden a giraffe?"

"No, they haven't, Sherilyn. I don't know why that is.

Maybe they're not as intelligent as horses. Certainly they wouldn't be as comfortable."

Martine stayed quiet, thinking to herself: If only they knew! If only they could see me and Jemmy racing across Sawubona's plains in the moonlight!

"Maybe it's because they're too stupid," said Lucy, with a sly glance at Martine. "I mean, it's not as if they do anything. They don't hunt or build nests or webs or have any purpose that I can see. All they do is stroll around and look pretty."

Instantly Martine's temper flared. "They *do* have a purpose," she snapped, turning on Lucy. "They act as lookouts for the other animals. They're very intelligent and have incredible eyesight and hearing, and they warn other animals if a predator is approaching. Their ears are so amazing they can even hear whistles that only dogs can usually hear."

As soon as it was out of her mouth, she regretted saying it, but it was too late to take it back.

"How do you know?" challenged Luke. "About the whistle, I mean."

"I just know, okay?" answered Martine, anxious to change the subject. "I read it in a book or something."

In the last row of the class, Xhosa stopped playing computer games and sat up straight.

"Miss Volkner," he said, "if Martine knows so much about giraffes, how come she hasn't told us about the white one that's supposed to live at Sawubona?"

"The one in the legend?" asked Miss Volkner. "Is this

true, Martine? I didn't know there was anything in it. You mean there actually is a white giraffe?"

Martine went red. "The white giraffe doesn't exist," she said. "Everyone knows that."

Heading off for a swimming lesson afterward, Martine felt shaken and guilty. The bad feeling that had come over her when she let slip the remark about the whistle returned with a vengeance. She tried to console herself with the thought that the only people who'd heard her say it were a bunch of hair gel and pop music obsessed kids—and Miss Volkner, who was a vegetarian—and they were hardly likely to go out hunting for the white giraffe. She was also relieved that she had already taken off the whistle in preparation for going swimming. And yet the butterflies continued to boil away in her stomach.

It was a Friday afternoon and the school was almost empty when Martine finally returned to her locker. She tried again to find the little watercolor, but with no success. She opened the door and stood staring in, frowning slightly. Again she had the feeling that someone had been tampering with her things. Out of the corner of her eye, she saw Gwyn Thomas's car pull into the parking lot. Martine removed her backpack and empty lunch box from the top shelf and hung her wet towel around her neck. She knew that she was keeping her grandmother waiting, but she continued to stare into her locker. The longer she stood there, the more feverish and worried she felt. Something else was missing; she was sure of it.

It wasn't until she was halfway back to Sawubona that it hit her.

The whistle was gone.

20

Martine tossed and turned all night and woke bleary-eyed at dawn. She felt sick. Not only had the whistle been stolen, but someone had changed the combination on the game park gate so she couldn't get in to find Jemmy. And that was not all. At some point in that awful night, she'd opened her window and leaned out into the wild wind, hoping to catch a glimpse of the white giraffe, and had seen instead a swoop of white light. Seconds later, darkness blanketed the game reserve again, but by then she was sure that the poachers were back and that they wouldn't be leaving without the white giraffe.

As scared as she was, Martine had forced herself to dress quickly and tiptoe down the stairs and out the front door.

Outside, the wind buffeted her and stung her skin, and the trees tossed like ocean waves. Martine ran barefoot down the sandy track that led to Tendai's house. Apart from Grace, there was nobody else she trusted to help her. The animals in the orphanage skittered in their cages as she passed, and she wished she could stop and soothe them. But every minute wasted would give the poachers more time to get away, so she ran on, thankful when the lights of Tendai's front porch shone through the swaying trees. Panting, she rang the bell. Nobody answered. That's when she noticed that the door was partially ajar. She pushed it with a finger and it opened.

"Tendai," Martine called. "Tendai, are you awake?"

But the house was silent. The bed hadn't been slept in and the remnants of a half-eaten meal lay on the table, as though the tracker had left in a hurry. When she checked around the back, his jeep was gone.

Martine sank onto a garden bench, defeated. So perhaps Tendai was involved after all. She walked on wooden legs back to the house, undressed, and climbed weakly under the covers. She wished she were brave enough to wake her grandmother and admit everything, but she couldn't face it. She'd been through too much. She just hid under the covers, feeling like a coward, and hoped that it would all go away. When sleep finally came, she was haunted by nightmares in which Tendai and the Five Star Gang were in cahoots and they were chasing her through a forest. The branches were catching fire as she ran, and she knew that they'd only rescue her if she told them where to find the white giraffe.

So she confessed, and they just laughed and left her to face the fire anyway.

In the harsh light of morning, the nightmare seemed more real than ever. Martine imagined Jemmy hearing the silent whistle and trustingly following the sound to his doom, and felt like the worst, most evil person on earth. She wanted to die. The most horrific images kept going through her mind. She saw Jemmy being skinned and used as a rug in some rich man's home, or being whipped and made to perform tricks in a circus, or even freezing to death in some Siberian zoo.

Worst of all, it was her fault. The secret of the white giraffe had been hers to keep, and it was her carelessness that had given it away. There was no reason for her to take the whistle to school, let alone the little watercolor of Jemmy. How could she have been so stupid? It was almost as if she'd wanted to be found out; wanted everyone to know that she was the girl in the legend, the one who could ride the white giraffe. After years of being an outsider, it was her chance to be special.

Now *special* was the very last thing she felt.

Martine decided that she had to leave Sawubona immediately. She didn't deserve to be there. She would go back to England on the first flight available—she would stow away if she had to—and Mr. Grice could find her a bed in an orphanage.

There was a knock at the door. "Martine?"

"Go away!" shouted Martine, burying her face in her pillow. "I'm not going to school."

The door opened and her grandmother came in. She sat down on the edge of the bed. "I know," she said quietly.

Martine took the pillow off her face. "You *know*?"

"Yes, I do. I know about the white giraffe. And if I'd told you that sooner, none of this would have happened."

Martine's heart skipped a beat. "Has something happened?"

Gwyn Thomas gave a heavy sigh and handed Martine a strand of silver tail hair. "Tendai found this tangled in the game park gate. Last night he received a hoax call from a man claiming to be a passerby, who said he had seen some buffaloes breaking through a hole in the game fence and that they were loose on the road. When Tendai got there, there was no hole and no buffalo. It was a trick to get him out of the way. He spent an hour searching for them before racing back to the reserve, but by then it was already too late. I'm sorry to have to tell you, Martine, the white giraffe is gone."

She stood up and walked around the bed to the window. "You see, Martine, you were right to be angry with me that night you wanted to know about your mother. There *are* too many secrets at Sawubona. But I thought I was protecting you. I thought I was protecting the white giraffe too. But now it seems I've done everything wrong." She turned to Martine. "I'm so sorry I've hurt you," she said.

Martine didn't know what was going on, but she was so relieved someone was still speaking to her that she jumped out of bed and took her grandmother's hand.

"It's okay," she said. "It's okay. But I don't understand what you mean about the giraffe. This is all *my* fault."

Her grandmother was silent for a long time. When she finally looked up, her face was etched with sorrow. "Sit down," she said. "There's something I need to tell you."

After Martine had made herself comfortable, her grandmother went out of the room and returned with tea and hot buttered English muffins and a large package, which she tucked between the bed and the table. Only when she was sure Martine had eaten her fill would Gwyn Thomas go on. She started by taking a present from the package and handing it to Martine.

"I've been meaning to give this to you since the day you came to Sawubona," she said, "but somehow there never was the right moment."

Martine took it from her with a puzzled frown and unwrapped it carefully. Inside was a heavy rectangular scrapbook crafted from handmade paper and pressed with wildflowers of the Cape. "It's beautiful," she told her grandmother.

She opened it. On the first page was a series of photos of a little girl with wavy brown hair and sparkling green eyes, playing with a lion cub.

"My mum," breathed Martine. On the next page was a poem Veronica had written, followed by pictures of her riding horses through the reserve at Sawubona, taking a curtain call in the school play, and splashing in the waves. There were wedding photos and holiday photos of Veronica and David, arms around each other, laughing, in the early days of their marriage. And on the final page, there was a picture of her mum and dad standing in front of the house at Sawubona, cradling a tiny baby.

"That's you," Gwyn Thomas said.

Martine's whole world shifted on its axis. "I was born in *Africa*?"

"You were born at Sawubona."

"Then why . . . ?"

"That's where your story begins," her grandmother said. "You see, Martine, the night after you came into the world Grace came to tell us that she'd had a vision that you were the child in the African legend, the one who has power over all the animals. She said that in years to come a white giraffe would be born on Sawubona and that fate would ensure you were brought together. That you were twin souls."

A faint smile tugged at her grandmother's lips. "Well, you can probably imagine our reaction. Grace has always had the gift of second sight, but we'd never actually heard her predict the future before, and somehow this just sounded so far-fetched. So initially, we were skeptical and then we were just amused. Veronica giggled and said she couldn't wait to see the faces of the other mothers at the Pony Club when her daughter turned up on a white giraffe.

"But Grace became angry and told her that it was not a joke. She led us to the window and there we saw a spectacle I will never forget as long as I live. Lions and zebras, leopards and springboks and other animals that usually prey on each other or fight with each other were lined up against the fence in perfect harmony, and they were looking toward the house. It was as if they knew something. After that, we took Grace very seriously. She said that along with the power—what she called the gift—would come enormous responsibility, and that although it would bring much beauty and happiness into your life, you would also experience great hardship and danger.

"Well, your mother was furious. She was afraid to believe what Grace was saying, but she was more afraid to ignore it. What made it even harder for her was that Grace insisted that sooner or later you would have to follow your destiny, whether you wanted to or not. Well, Veronica refused to accept that."

Martine was spellbound. "So what happened next?"

"After talking it over with your father, your mother decided that she could stop the course of destiny by taking you away from Africa, keeping you away from animals and severing all ties with Sawubona.

"Your grandfather and I were devastated, but we understood her reasons—she was convinced it was the only way to keep you from danger—and we also felt that there was a chance the plan might work. So that's what we did. Within two or three days of your birth, as soon as you were able to travel, you went to England."

"It must have been very hard for you," Martine pressed. "Saying good-bye to my mum and dad and knowing you might never see them again."

"It was the hardest thing I've ever done," her grandmother said with feeling. "But for a long time it was worth it because Veronica was so happy. She believed—we all believed—that it had worked. Then four months ago, shortly before Christmas, I went to Grace's house for dinner. When I got there she was reading the bones—Africans with second sight throw bones the way Western fortune-tellers use crystal balls and tarot cards—and she answered the door in such a state, perspiring and talking gibberish, that I thought she had a fever. She said the bones had told her that a tragedy would bring you back to Sawubona. She wanted me to phone Veronica right then and say anything, even lie and say I was ill if I had to, just to bring you all back to Sawubona. She said that if you came of your own accord, the gods might be appeased and the tragedy would be averted.

"Of course, I was very alarmed. It was hard not to be. But I tried to reason with her. I said that perhaps the bones were mistaken and that, apart from the fact that I had no intention of lying to my own daughter, she could hardly expect a whole family to move continents for a second time on the basis of her visions. After all, we'd seen no evidence at all that the first one might come true. We ended up having a terrible fight over it. She was my friend, but we haven't spoken since. She was always adamant that you shouldn't be taken away from here. She kept saying that the forefathers had predicted your coming. I just told her she was mad. To be truthful, I really hoped she *was* mad."

Gwyn Thomas took a ragged breath and for the first time since coming to Sawubona, Martine understood the extent of her grandmother's loss. She squeezed her hand and was rewarded with a grateful smile.

"So I told your mother what she'd said," Gwyn Thomas went on. "For Veronica, it was the last straw. She said that for years she'd had to suffer the heartache of being away from me, her dad, and her beloved Africa. Finally, she'd found happiness. David had a good job, you were growing up wonderfully, and you all had lots of plans for the future. She was not about to uproot you a second time for what would probably, in the end, turn out to be nothing more than superstitious babbling.

"It was the last time we spoke. Days later, I received a call to say that your mum and dad had lost their lives in a house fire. I blamed myself. I felt that if only I'd worked harder to convince them to leave, it would never have happened. Then the will was read and I was told I was your sole relative. We had always agreed that I wouldn't be your guardian if your parents died, because that would mean you would have to return to Africa. But the will had recently been changed. Why Veronica changed her mind, we'll never know. It seemed the cruelest of ironies. After everything we'd done to keep you away from Sawubona, you were destined to return after all."

Martine suddenly realized she had been holding her

breath. "Phew! Now I understand why you didn't want me to come here."

"Yes," said her grandmother. "And I feel very ashamed about the way I've treated you. At first, I must admit I resented you. Every time I looked at you, it reminded me that it was because of you that your mother had gone away and I hadn't seen her for eleven years. Later, I was afraid to get close to you. I thought that if I loved you and you were taken away from me, it would be like losing Veronica all over again."

"You're not the only one who lost my mum," Martine said pointedly.

"I realize that now. But by the time I came to my senses, I had already driven you away."

"I haven't been driven away," Martine assured her. "Maybe we could start again."

Her grandmother touched her hand. "You're very wise. No wonder the forefathers chose you."

At those words, Martine suddenly recalled the ghastly events of the night.

"But what about Jemmy?" she fretted. "What did you mean about protecting Jemmy?"

Her grandmother looked confused.

"Jeremiah. *The giraffe!*"

"Of course! Well, a few days after the poachers attacked your grandfather, the local Zulu chief came to see me. He told me that in the hours before the hunters arrived at Sawubona our female giraffe had given birth to a snow-white calf. She and her mate later died trying to protect him, but somehow—it might even have been because Henry arrived to distract the men—the baby giraffe managed to get away in the struggle. According to the chief, it was rescued by an elephant whose own calf had been stillborn and she had taken it to a secret place. The chief said that the giraffe had special powers and that it was the rarest animal on earth. On no account should anyone ever find out about it. He said that if anyone ever asked me about it, I had to deny it existed. I couldn't even tell Tendai or your mother. And when you came I tried everything in my power to keep the two of you apart so that the prophecy would not be fulfilled."

"Grandmother, Jemmy is my best friend," Martine confessed.

"I won't ask how the two of you became so close," her grandmother remarked dryly. "I suppose that explains why your clothes are always covered in mud and strange grasses these days, and why you're always yawning on the way in to school."

"I'm sorry," Martine said. "I didn't think you'd understand. And now it's because of me that Jemmy has been stolen. Somehow I have to try to find him. Grandmother, do you think you might be able to help me?"

"No," said Gwyn Thomas. "But I know someone who can."

21

The pale green house looked exactly the way Martine remembered it. The rusting Coca-Cola sign was propped against one wall, the lawn was even more threadbare, and the chickens were still scratching hopefully on the porch in the sunshine. It was mid-April and Martine found it hard to believe that barely three months had passed since she had climbed off the plane at Cape Town airport. It felt like forever. She remembered Grace's words on the first day: "The gift can be a blessing or a curse. Make your decisions wisely." The sick feeling returned to Martine's stomach. Her decisions might have cost Jemmy his life.

A small boy materialized at the front door. "I'd like a

word with that crazy old woman," said Gwyn Thomas. "Is she home?"

"Who you be callin' crazy?" purred Grace, looming up behind the boy. "There's only one crazy old woman round these parts and that'd be Gwyn Thomas." She reached out a massive hand and stroked Martine's hair, giving no indication that she'd seen her only recently. "Chile looks like she could use summa Grace's good food. What you been feeding her?"

"We haven't come here to be insulted," Martine's grandmother said primly. "We need your help."

"Uh-huh," said Grace, putting her hands on her hips. "I be listenin'."

"Grace, I know we've had our differences," Gwyn Thomas said. "I don't blame you if you never want to speak to me again. But if you ever cared for me at all, you'll help Martine. She's lost something she loves and you may be the only person in the world who can help her to get it back."

Grace smiled, revealing a lot of pink gum and very few teeth. "Old woman," she said, "why didn't you just say so?"

Without ceremony, she turned and walked back into the house. Martine and her grandmother followed the swish of Grace's dress, a riotous blend of indigo, sunshine yellow, and burnt honey, patterned with African prints. She led them to the living room, which smelled familiarly of chopped wood, mealie-meal, and a million cooking fires. The out-of-date island calendar was still on the wall and the same grass mat was on the floor. A vase full of peacock feathers had been added to a teak table.

Grace went into the kitchen and reappeared with two steaming plates of mealie-meal porridge drenched with buttermilk, cinnamon, and cane sugar. Martine was queasy and not at all keen on eating, but Grace stifled her protests with a flat, "You're arl bones."

Afterward, Martine was glad that she had. The porridge was fantastic. It poured into her veins like molten lava, warming her bones and clearing her head. When she was finished, Martine told Grace what had happened to Jemmy, giving her as much detail as she could about the poachers' chase.

"One question, chile," Grace said when she had finished. "Did you ever see the face of any of them hunters?"

Martine glanced uneasily at her grandmother.

"Go on," urged Gwyn Thomas.

"Well, I didn't see either of their faces, but I think that somebody at Sawubona might be involved. I think it could be . . ." Martine faltered. She didn't want to make her grandmother angry again.

"It could be Alex," she said at last.

"No!" cried her grandmother. "Your grandfather trusted Alex with his life. I won't have you saying—"

"ENOUGH!" commanded Grace. "The chile has spoken. Now we must listen for the answers."

She heaved herself off the chair and drew the curtains. The room was plunged into blackness. A match flared and Grace placed a candle on the table. She sat down on the grass mat with a grunt, her broad face and deep-set eyes glittering eerily. Out of her blouse she produced a small leather pouch, which she proceeded to empty on the ground in front of her. As far as Martine could tell, it contained a collection of small bones, a portion of porcupine quill, a guinea fowl feather, and a couple of elephant hairs. Grace closed her eyes and began to chant.

Nothing happened for several minutes and then a low, rhythmic pounding began to emanate from Grace's chest, like the sound of a distant drum. Before Martine's startled eyes, a thin spiral of blue smoke rose from the objects on the floor. It flattened out and blurred images began to flash across it, too fast for her to take in. There were mountains and men in loincloths and headdresses, great herds of animals and bloody battles, and once she thought she saw a giraffe, but it was gone before she could be sure.

Grace's eyes rolled back in her head. "Water," she moaned. "I see blue, blue water and boats that go up to the sky. The men are going far. They be hungry for the power. The white giraffe is there, but not for much longer. I see much pain, much pain, much pain . . ."

"Stop!" shouted Gwyn Thomas.

The smoke disappeared. Grace's eyes swam back into her head. She was shaking. She looked up at Martine.

"Go now, chile. Soon it will be too late."

"But where?" cried Martine. "Where have they taken him?"

"'Boats that go up to the sky' can only mean one thing—the dockyards in Cape Town," interrupted her grandmother. "Hurry, Martine. I think they're taking him abroad."

158

22

Maybe Gwyn Thomas had driven as fast as she did on the way into Cape Town before that day, but Martine seriously doubted it. As it was, the needle on the ancient red Datsun quivered as if it were about to burst through the glass. Martine could tell that her grandmother was very anxious. But she was also very determined. She had agreed to drive Martine to the docks but no farther. "If Jeremiah isn't there, we'll have to call the police," she'd said firmly. All Martine's protests had been in vain.

The two hours that it took to reach the ocean seemed the longest of Martine's life. Every possible obstacle conspired to delay them. A police roadblock. A traffic jam. A busload of disembarking senior citizens. Three loose cows ambling across the road.

And all the while Grace's prophecy kept running through Martine's head. *The white giraffe is there, but not for much longer. I see much pain, much pain, much pain . . .*

They were on an inland road and soon the wine estates, with their pristine white Cape Dutch buildings and lavender-lined drives, were followed by shantytowns reminiscent of the Soweto Tendai had described to Martine. Mile upon mile of rusting iron and water-stained plywood shacks, worm-ridden dogs, and shifty, hungry-eyed youths. Children played in the dirt with wire toys. The thought of Tendai brought back the memory of the day they'd spent together at Sawubona.

Gwyn Thomas pulled off the highway and took the coastal road down to the waterfront. The forbidding crags of Table Mountain were draped in thick cloud. When tall gray cargo ships and cranes lifting containers came into view, she slowed the car to a crawl. Martine was ready to explode with impatience, but she knew that they had to find a place to hide the car. An overgrown track provided a solution. They bounced over the weeds and stones and parked under a flat-topped pine tree. Gwyn Thomas opened her door and started to get out of the car. Martine put her hand on her grandmother's sleeve.

"Grandmother. This is something I have to do on my own."

"I don't think so," Gwyn Thomas said wryly. "You're

eleven years old and you're an hour and a half from home."

But Martine stood her ground. "It's my fault that Jemmy's been captured, and if he's hurt, that'll be my fault too. I've got to be the one to try to find him."

Gwyn Thomas sat back down and closed the car door. A battle was going on behind her eyes. "Where is this all going to end?" she said, and Martine had a feeling that she was talking about much more than the disappearance of the giraffe.

She put a hand on Martine's shoulder. "All right, go and look for your precious Jemmy. But if you're not back in forty-five minutes, I'm calling the police. I'm not taking any chances. The pain of losing one child was terrible. I couldn't bear it if I lost another."

Martine leaned forward and gave her a kiss on the cheek, and was surprised to see her grandmother's blue eyes fill with tears.

"Thanks for everything," she said.

She hopped out of the car and ran back along the track to the main road. The ocean wind cut through her thin T-shirt like a knife and the salty air tingled in her nostrils. At the bottom of the hill, behind a high fence fortified with coils of razor wire, lay the shipyard. Beyond it, the sea was a churning, white-capped green. The shipyard was buzzing with activity and she could hear dogs barking— guard dogs, perhaps. Martine waited shivering behind a tree for a couple of cars to pass. She was beginning to regret that she hadn't brought a jacket. She put a hand on the medicine pouch that Grace had given her at the Secret

Valley. In the car, her grandmother had commented on it, but Martine would say nothing about it except that it had been a gift from a friend to bring her luck. Now she drew courage from it. She had also brought along Mr. Morrison's Swiss Army knife for good measure. If she could get to Jemmy, she was sure that she could help him.

When the road was clear, she sprinted to the gate and slipped behind the wooden guardhouse. She'd intended to try to talk her way in, but when she peered through the salt-smeared window, there didn't seem any real need. There were two security men in the hut. One was watching rugby on TV and stirring a cup of tea, his chair balancing precariously on its rear legs. The other was on his radio, his back toward the window. He was having an argument. "Who're you calling an idiot? Over."

Furious crackling followed.

Martine didn't wait to hear any more. She ducked under the barrier and ran for the mountainous lines of blue, red, and gray containers. With every stride she expected to hear voices yelling for her to stop, but no one seemed to notice her. Except . . .

A snarl that almost turned her blood to yogurt brought her to a terrified halt. A rottweiler was blocking her path, his lips pulled back over teeth as savage and numerous as a crocodile's. In spite of the icy breeze, Martine began to sweat. Instinctively she fixed her green eyes on the rottweiler's big yellow ones and focused all her energy on dominating him, telling him that if he dared to prevent her from saving Jemmy, she'd personally feed him to the sharks.

Then she commanded him to lie down and let her pass.

To her astonishment, the rottweiler sank to the ground with a piteous whine. He put his paws over his eyes. If Martine hadn't been so scared, she would have laughed.

She stepped over him and sneaked forward until she came to a gap between two metal containers. Through it, she could see the docks. There were three gray ships and a blue and white tugboat in the harbor. The shipyard itself was bustling with workers. Martine estimated that there were about twenty-five crates and several expensive cars in the process of being loaded. There was no sign of a giraffe. Time was running out for Jemmy and she didn't know where to start. How could she even begin to search three ships the size of skyscrapers? What had she been thinking? Why hadn't she just called the police as her grandmother suggested? Why did she always have to do everything the hard way? Why was she always so stubborn?

Suddenly she was grabbed from behind. "Let go of me," she screeched, and began to fight and squeal like a wounded warthog. She and her assailant hit the ground with a thud. Martine lay on her stomach, groaning, too winded to move.

"I'm arresting you for trespassing on private property," said a clear young voice. "You have the right to remain silent . . ."

Martine rolled over, still breathing heavily.

"You!" she cried.

A pair of lion's eyes gazed calmly back at her. "Hello, Martine," Ben said, grinning.

23

Martine scrambled to her feet, ignoring the hand Ben held out to her.

"You could have been a bit more gentle with me," she said crossly.

"I apologize," said Ben, who seemed to be struggling not to laugh. "I didn't recognize you until we were in midair. But you *are* trespassing, you know."

"What about you?" Martine accused. "Isn't that what you're doing?"

"My father is a sailor." Ben pointed to one of the tall gray ships. "That's his boat over there—the *Aurora*. I have permission to be here. You don't."

Martine sighed. She could see that she had no choice

164

but to tell Ben about Jemmy and just pray that he didn't try to stop her. As briefly and quickly as she could, she explained about her betrayal of the white giraffe, about the hunters, and about Grace's prediction. She also told him about her grandmother, parked behind the pines, waiting. Lastly, she told him how much Jemmy meant to her and how desperate she was to save him.

"Please, Ben," she said, "please say you won't stand in my way."

Ben's face was serious. "For ages now my father has worried that his ship is being used to smuggle rare animals out of the country, but he didn't want to notify the authorities until he was sure. If the giraffe is on board, I think we can get to him, but we must go at once. The *Aurora* sets sail in thirty minutes."

Before Martine could get used to this new Ben—a Ben who spoke and smiled and was a million miles away from the shy, studious boy he appeared to be at school—he was striding confidently across the shipyard, beckoning for her to follow. He wore ragged jeans, heavy boots, and a sleeveless black T-shirt, and his arms, though thin, were sinewy and strong. Martine ran to catch up with him.

"What do you think you're doing?" she inquired breathlessly. "Do you really imagine that we are just going to walk onto the ship and walk off with a giraffe?"

"*We* aren't," said Ben. "*You* are." He smiled. "Trust me. Sometimes the most obvious way is the best way."

As if to prove him right, a commotion erupted on

the jetty. A crate had broken while it was being hoisted onto the deck, and what looked like an antique table and several highly polished chairs were bobbing around in the greasy green harbor. Men were cursing and shaking their fists and two guard dogs were going berserk at the end of their chains. Ben took no notice of them. He strode coolly across the gangplank of the ship, onto the deck, and through a low doorway. Martine scuttled in after him.

Below deck, the ship was a warren of corridors, galleys, and anonymous cabins. They walked as quickly as they could along miles of battleship-gray passages and down two spiral staircases, their footsteps ringing like church bells on the steel. Finally they came to a storage room. A swarthy man was hunched over a computer. He jumped up when Ben tapped at the door and shouted something in a foreign language.

Ben gave him a radiant smile. "Captain Holloway is asking for you up on deck," he said politely. "I'm not sure what it's about, but it seems to be urgent."

The man glared at him suspiciously. He reached for his radio.

"I'm pretty sure it's an emergency," Ben said again.

Muttering, the man snatched up some papers and scurried away along the corridor. Ben waited until he was out of sight and then darted into the room.

"Martine! In here!"

He locked the door behind them and opened a filing cabinet. In it, hanging from brass hooks, were hundreds of keys. He began to sort through them methodically, laying them on the floor. Martine checked her watch. It was just after midday. The boat sailed in twenty minutes. She dreaded to imagine the consequences if they hadn't found Jemmy by then.

There was a knock at the door. Ben put his finger to his lips. The knock turned into hammering. Martine was a nervous wreck. Ben remained perfectly serene. He examined each key meticulously, as if he had several spare hours up his sleeve, seemingly unconcerned that he was participating in an illegal animal rescue, or that a raging Russian was now attacking the door with what sounded like a fire extinguisher. The pounding ceased and there was the steel echo of footsteps running away.

"Please!!" Martine panicked.

"Got it," said Ben, holding up a bunch of keys. "But we don't have much time."

He unlocked the door and the two of them shot across the passageway and down two more spiral staircases, darting into a supply closet when a couple of grease-stained engineers popped out of a side door. Martine judged that they were now on the bottom of the ship. The air reeked with fumes. The floor shuddered and there was the low grinding roar of great engines coming to life.

"Do you think we're going to make it?" whispered Martine.

Ben didn't answer. They had reached an intersection of corridors and he was trying to decide which way to go.

167

"Oy, oy," thundered a voice. "What have we here?"

Out of the gloom came a sun-reddened man with immaculately cut gray hair. He was marching toward them with a ferocious expression on his face.

"Good afternoon, sir," Ben called out cheerfully.

The man's demeanor changed. "Good heavens, Ben," he said, "I didn't realize it was you." He looked at Martine and frowned. "The two of you shouldn't really be down here, you know. This section is supposed to be off-limits, and we're sailing in fifteen minutes."

"I'm so sorry, sir. I was showing my friend Martine around the ship and I lost track of time. I must admit I'm also a little bit lost."

"That's not like you, Ben," chuckled the man. "You know this boat almost as well as your father does. If you take that passage to the cargo section, you'll find an elevator going up to the deck. Hurry now. You don't want to end up in Kazakhstan. Ha ha!"

Ben thanked him profusely and they ran off down the corridor. Soon they came to a large steel door. A red-lettered sign warned staff that they entered at their own risk and disclaimed any responsibility for injuries, psychological trauma, or death caused by the biting, kicking or venomous inhabitants within.

Ben pressed the keys into Martine's hand.

"This is as far as I go. It's more than my father's job is worth for me to be caught down here. When you come out, take the elevator up to level three and cross the gangplank. As soon as you're on the jetty, look left. You'll see a path leading up the hill to a pair of tall gates. I'll make sure they're open."

Martine hesitated. There was one more thing. "Do you think you could try to get a message to my grandmother?"

Ben nodded. "It's a promise. Good luck. You're on your own now."

It took Martine five tries to find the right key. And all the while the ship creaked, seethed, and groaned like a wounded beast. Once or twice, Martine was convinced she felt it shift in its moorings. Finally, the lock clicked. She wrestled open the heavy steel door, feeling hopeful for the first time that day. As she entered, a nail caught her T-shirt sleeve and ripped a small hole in it. She pulled herself free, barely noticing it.

As soon as the door hissed shut behind her, the stench of oil, animals, manure, and seawater came at her in a sickly wave. She was in a cramped container area lit with flickering neon tubes. Scores of crates and boxes, many draped with tarpaulins, were stacked in untidy rows in the shadows. Martine rushed over to those nearest to her and peered inside. There were glass cases full of writhing snakes, cages crammed with crestfallen parrots, and boxes full of whimpering monkeys. A huddle of depressed sheep cowered in a crate that was plainly too small for them. The last container on the row housed an enormous blue-bottomed male baboon. When she lifted up the cover, the baboon lunged at the bars of his cage, yellow teeth bared. Martine almost jumped out of her skin.

There was no sign of the giraffe.

Martine had never felt more helpless in her life. Her heart ached for all these creatures that had been treated with less regard than a shipment of coal or rice. As if they had no feelings or needs. As if they were immune to thirst or hunger and impervious to pain. But she knew that there was no way on earth for her to save them all now. It was looking increasingly unlikely that she'd even find Jemmy.

She tried to think logically. There were no obvious labels on the containers, but that didn't mean they weren't marked in some way. There had to be a system of identifying them. She studied the boxes nearest to her. Each had a number scribbled on the lower right-hand side of the door. A twinge on her upper arm reminded her of the nail that had torn her sleeve. Something had been swinging from it. Some sort of notebook? Seconds later she had it: No. 144, giraffe, Aisle C.

She saw No. 144 right away. And if she'd been thinking more clearly, she'd probably have spotted it sooner. It was a black-painted container, higher and wider than the rest. She dashed over to it and whipped the tarpaulin aside. Jemmy was lying on the floor, his legs at odd angles. His white and silver coat was covered in cuts and matted blood. He seemed to be dead.

170

"Jemmy!" sobbed Martine. "Oh, Jemmy. What have I done to you?"

Jemmy raised his head at the sound of her voice. His eyes were dull and empty.

Martine fell on her knees beside the container. "Jemmy, please don't die. I love you so much."

The white giraffe flopped down again and his eyelids drooped. His breathing was shallow. Martine slid back bolts on the cage door and knelt down beside him. She began to stroke his face and neck, feeling again the now familiar tingle.

"Please wake up, Jemmy. Please."

There was no response.

Martine closed her eyes and put her hands on the white giraffe's heart. Unbidden, Technicolor memories of their time together came flooding into her mind. Of the evening she first saw him, standing in the storm, shimmering against the night sky. Of the unforgettable moment when he rested his head on her shoulder. Of lying on his back high up on the escarpment, staring at the Milky Way. Of their exhilarating rides among the hippos, elephants, and lions of Sawubona.

Through it all, Martine was aware of her hands becoming hotter and hotter and a pure feeling, like love, flowing through her.

A huge shudder went through Jemmy's body. He gave a great gasping breath, as if trying to reclaim the life that had nearly been taken from him. His eyes opened at the same time as Martine's. The light came back into them and Martine knew in that moment that he still loved her and still had faith in her.

Martine pressed her face against his velvety shoulder and gave him a kiss. She sat up. Fingers trembling, she fumbled in the pouch for one of the bottles that Grace had given her on the night they'd met in the cave. "For bleedin' or to numb any pain," she'd instructed. Privately, Martine had resolved never to use it. It was the most alarming color, and the smell of it—somewhere between minced-up frogs and Brussels sprouts—made her want to vomit. But right now she had very few options. She knew she had the power to heal, but she wasn't yet sure how much her gift could do. She'd gotten the impression from what had happened with the kudu that she still needed the help of traditional medicine in certain situations. Martine didn't know how badly injured Jemmy was or even if he was capable of walking, but she did know that they had no chance of getting out of the shipyard unless he could gallop. She removed the cork from the bottle and, holding her nose with one hand, daubed the mixture onto his cuts with the other. It sizzled on application.

The ship gave a lurch that almost sent her flying. She held her watch up to the light. Only six minutes till they sailed.

Martine was frantic. The mixture would have to work its magic along the way. She stroked the white giraffe urgently. "Jemmy," she said, "we have to go." After what seemed an eternity, he lumbered to his feet and stood there swaying.

Martine started for the door and breathed a sigh of thanks when he followed her, stumbling a little.

They were almost at the exit when a glint of gold and black caught Martine's eye. Leopard cubs! Martine was pretty sure that they, too, had been stolen from Sawubona. They could even be the cubs whose spoor Tendai had shown her at the escarpment. But even if they were, there was no way she could help them now. They were lying in a heap in the corner of their cage, clearly drugged.

With a last anguished look at the cubs, Martine guided Jemmy through the steel door and into the cargo elevator. It was at least three times the width and depth of a normal elevator, but the giraffe still had to bend his neck. He snorted with alarm. Martine pressed the button for level three and the elevator began to rise. She realized then that she hadn't thought past the point of rescuing him. With Martine on foot and the white giraffe running fear-crazed around the dockyard, pursued no doubt by men with guns, disaster would quickly follow. She would have to ride him.

Jemmy was quaking in the clattering, claustrophobic elevator, but he stood quietly when she indicated that she was going to try to mount him. Using the support rail as a foothold and doing everything she could to avoid touching any of the cuts on his neck or shoulders, Martine scrambled onto his back just as the elevator shuddered to a halt. One minute to go. The doors opened. Alex du Preez was standing in front of them, talking on his cell phone.

"In the end, it was much easier than we thought," he was saying. "Like taking candy from a baby."

He saw Martine and Jemmy at the same moment they saw him. His face went the color of a frozen turkey. He dropped his phone and whirled around. "Raise the gangplank!" he roared. "Stop them!!"

"Run, Jemmy!" screamed Martine, but the white giraffe was already in full flight. He swept across the deck, striking Alex a glancing blow with his hoof as he went. Alex dropped like a stone. There was a loud grinding noise and the gangplank began to rise. On the jetty, men were shouting and pointing and tearing across the dockyard from all directions. The ship began to move. Martine's heart was ready to burst out of her chest, but Jemmy never hesitated. He galloped up the gangplank as it rose and took a flying leap. Martine looked down. There was nothing below them but ocean.

24

The first thing Martine noticed when she and Jemmy crashed down onto the jetty was the police cars. They were streaming through the shipyard gates in a blizzard of flashing lights and sirens. The second thing she saw was the path leading up the hill.

"That way!" she cried.

Jemmy had stumbled when he landed and then swerved to avoid the guard dogs, and Martine had nearly fallen off. Now she clung hard to his mane and gripped with her legs as he steadied himself and raced up the slope toward the iron gates. They were open, just as Ben had promised. As they galloped through, Martine caught a glimpse of Ben behind the wall. He

175

had an excited grin on his face and he was waving.

Martine lifted her hand and smiled back. "Thanks, Ben," she shouted, "I won't ever forget this."

As they left the shipyard it occurred to Martine that she didn't know the way to Sawubona. Nor had she given any thought to the complicated question of how to ride a wild animal through the traffic in Cape Town. But she needn't have worried. Jemmy was guided by the instincts of his ancestors to follow the sun on an unerring course for home. He never faltered. He turned away from the city, with its hooting cars and crowded beaches, jumped over a stream, and began to run as if his life depended on it. Which, in a way, it did.

For the first mile, Martine fully expected the police cars to come screaming over the horizon, but they didn't. Nothing interrupted the steady thud-thud of the giraffe's hooves. Apart from a brief pause for a drink when they crossed a rushing river, Jemmy ran without tiring, leaping fences whenever he came to them. Whatever Grace had put in the foul-smelling potion, it had worked a miracle.

They traveled inland, away from the suburbs and the stormy coast. Sometimes the landscape was nothing more than parched gray desert, with ostriches strutting jauntily through the scrub. At other times, low-slung hills gave way to valleys carpeted in wildflowers, purple mountains of protea, and heathery fynbos, or golden acres of wheat. They traveled so swiftly and so silently that few people saw them go by. And those who did either toppled over in a dead faint, checked their mugs of tea for alcohol content, or carried on about their business with little more than a shake of their head, convinced that their eyes were deceiving them.

Only when they reached the outskirts of Storm Crossing did Jemmy slow to a walk. The sun was still shining, but a fine misty rain had begun to fall. Martine had learned from Tendai that the Africans called these sunshowers "monkey's weddings," although he wasn't sure why. Ahead of them, Martine could see a crowd of people gathered. As they drew closer, people started coming out of their houses and shops and pointing and clapping, and once or twice Martine thought she heard cheering. She tried to persuade Jemmy to take a different route, but he turned down the main street. From the bakery onward, men, women, and children lined the street three deep. From her lofty perch, Martine could see for hundreds of yards in any direction, but there was no sign of any festival or passing parade. It was only when a group of little kids began chanting her name that she realized that all the fuss was for her and Jemmy.

Martine could hardly take it in. They passed a police car parked outside the post office. Alex was glowering in the back in handcuffs, a swollen purple egg on his forehead. He shot Martine a poisonous glance as she went by. A smartly dressed black man, whom Martine recognized from the newspapers as Xhosa Washington's father, was being led out of the mayor's office by two constables, protesting his innocence as he went. Behind the police car was Tendai's jeep. An outraged mewing was coming from inside. The leopard cubs, thought Martine, and she could have wept with gladness.

The jeep doors opened and Tendai emerged beaming and covered in scratches. When he saw the white giraffe and Martine riding high, he took off his hat and stared in amazement. "The white giraffe," he said. "So many times, I wished . . . I hoped . . . He's truly a creature of the gods, little one, like a horse made of stars."

Martine smiled down at him, tears of happiness in her eyes. The only thing missing now was her grandmother.

As if reading her mind, Tendai said, "Your grandmother is waiting at Sawubona for you, little one. She knew your friend would carry you home safely."

Martine thanked him and Tendai opened the jeep doors again to deal with the leopard cubs. Later, he would tell her that he'd suspected for a year that Alex was stealing animals from Sawubona, but he'd never come close to proving it.

"I just didn't want to believe it," he confided to Martine.

After Alex's arrest, detectives found that he was the mastermind of a massive poaching operation that had lasted nearly three years. During that time, he and his accomplices—one was Xhosa Washington's father, the mayor, who had processed the export licenses—had sent hundreds of animals, many of them rare, to collectors around the world, the main culprit being a billionaire from Kazakhstan. He wanted them for his private safari park. There, they were hunted and eaten at exotic feasts, or stuffed, and their heads and skins used to decorate his mansion walls. The poachers Alex had heroically caught at Sawubona were a rival gang that he was only too pleased to get rid of. He certainly hadn't done it to protect the animals.

When questioned, Alex was adamant that Martine's grandfather's death at Sawubona had been an accident, claiming that a gun had discharged when Henry was wrestling with another member of the gang. He insisted he'd patched Henry up as best he could before fleeing with the other men. He also said that he had taken the job at Sawubona in an "attempt to put things right." How Martine laughed when she heard that.

It would be some time, however, before any of this was known, and for now all Martine was aware of was that Jemmy and the leopard cubs were safe. She smiled so much, her cheeks hurt. When she caught sight of the Van Heerden twins ducking red-faced into an alleyway, embarrassed, no doubt, by the part she suspected they'd played in helping to steal the silent whistle, she began to laugh out loud.

What a difference a day makes, she thought to herself.

It was almost sundown by the time Jemmy turned in to the sandy road that led to Sawubona. Doves were cooing in the thorn trees and the air smelled the way it had on Martine's very first evening at the game reserve—of cooking fires, wild animals, and herby earth and trees. The fading sky was threaded with gold. Ahead of them was a perfect rainbow. It arched over Gwyn Thomas's thatched house and ended in the game park, close to the water hole. Martine had a lump in her throat. She and Jemmy had been through so much together. He was her best friend and her loyal protector, and she loved him more than anything else on the planet. But he needed his freedom. Once again, she was going to have to let him go.

When she reached the game park gate nearest to the house, Martine put her arms around Jemmy's neck and he lowered her to the ground. "Good-bye, my beautiful friend," she said. "I'll miss you."

But Jemmy refused to leave. He made his musical fluttering sound and pushed his nose against Martine's chest. She ran her hand over his silken mane and cinnamon-tinted patches. "I'll always be here if you need me, I promise," she said tenderly. "But right now you need some rest, and for that you need to go home to the Secret Valley."

Martine watched the white giraffe gallop away through the reserve until she could no longer see him. He'd be back, she was sure of it. She resumed her walk to the thatched house, where her grandmother was waiting.

As she approached the gate, she saw Grace. The *sangoma* was seated on a tree stump in her indigo, yellow, and burnt honey dress, wearing a matching headdress. She gave a pink-gummed smile, stretched out her arms, and swept Martine to her breast for an ecstatic squeeze. "You done well, chile. The forefathers, they be very proud of you," she said.

The last remaining dark cloud lifted from Martine's heart. "Thank you, Grace," she panted when she managed to extricate herself. "But I still feel very ashamed. I let everyone down. Jemmy trusted me and I behaved so stupidly."

"We arl make mistakes, chile. That's human. But not everybody has the courage to admit what they done and go out into the world to try to mend things. You be very brave. Like I told you, the gift can be a curse, not just a blessin'. When all was said and done, you made your decisions wisely."

"But Grace, surely this wasn't the reason I was chosen?" asked Martine. "I mean, I know I managed to save Jemmy, but it was my fault he was stolen in the first place."

"You're right, chile," replied Grace. "This ain't the task that you been chosen for. This be a test, nothin' more. There be many, many challenges to come. You will travel to the ends of the earth and have a whole lotta adventures before you're done.

"This is not the end, you see. This is only the beginning."

Author's Note

I'll start with a confession. Until a couple of years ago I had never, in quite a long career as a journalist and biographer, entertained the idea of writing a children's book, mainly because I've never been one of these people who thought that writing a children's book would be easy.

Then in December 2004, I was walking along a blustery street in London, England, when out of nowhere an image popped into my head of a girl on a giraffe. When I was a child I actually had a pet giraffe and I thought: Wouldn't it be the coolest thing on earth to be able to ride a giraffe? And right there on the street the entire story, right down to the girl's name, Martine, came into my head almost fully formed.

I went home and wrote it down. I thought: One day when I'm retired, I'll have a tinker with it. But soon after, I went to Africa for a safari on a game reserve, and the whole time I was there, the book was on my mind. When I returned to London, I was very busy with other projects but I decided that I'd spend a few hours every Saturday writing it. Well, the first Saturday came and I wrote the first chapter. It just came to me like I was watching a movie. After that, I found I couldn't stop doing it. I put my other projects aside and carried on!

And it was so much fun. I was writing the novel during a gray, rainy winter in London, but every morning I'd sit down at my computer and think: Where should I go today? And within seconds I could be sitting with, say, Martine and Tendai, the Zulu tracker at Sawubona, enjoying a campfire breakfast on an escarpment, looking down at a herd of buffalo and watching the sun come up over the African bush.

For me, the best part was being able to revisit the landscape of my childhood. When I was Martine's age, I lived on a farm, which was part game reserve, in Zimbabwe, which borders South Africa. Apart from our giraffe, Jenny, we had two cantankerous ostriches, a wildebeest, a herd of fifty or sixty impala antelope, and a troop of monkeys. As a family, we were animal crazy and so apart from hordes of cats, dogs, and horses, we were forever adopting stray goats or taking in wild orphans, like our two warthogs, Miss Piggy and Bacon.

For a long time I wanted to be a veterinarian. I had a "vet kit," which was full of bandages and syringes and various wound treatments that I used to patch up injured birds or antelope or other animals that were carried to our door. My father did a lot of non-emergency animal treatment on the farm, so I learned from him. Plus I read anything I could on the subject. Those experiences helped a great deal when I was thinking about Martine's gift of healing and the situations in which she might apply it.

Like Martine, I was fascinated with bushcraft. Because I spent a lot of time alone in the game reserve, I was constantly at risk of being bitten by snakes or chased by ostriches or even devoured by one of the crocodiles in the river beside our house. I was always on the lookout for survival tips. There's a scene in the book where Martine uses soldier termites to stitch up a wound, and that's something I've actually tried, although using a leaf rather than a living creature. It works!

The reason I set the story in Cape Town, South Africa,

rather than Zimbabwe, is because I wanted the best of both worlds—the awesome scenery of the Cape, with its ocean and mountains and vineyards, and the savannah of Zimbabwe. In South Africa, real savannah occurs much farther north than I've located it, but the best part about being a novelist is that you can move things around! Thus, Storm Crossing, where Martine lives, is a fictional town about two hours from Cape Town, and Sawubona has a mix of savannah and fynbos, a plant kingdom unique to the Cape.

Grace and Tendai are composites of Africans I've known. I sometimes feel that if the only experience a person ever had of Africa was what they saw or heard on the news, they could be forgiven for thinking that the whole continent was mired in disease, famine, and conflict. It is true that large sections of it do suffer from those things, but in between are areas of breathtaking beauty, rare and amazing wildlife, and beautiful, talented, giving people, like Tendai and Grace.

In African culture, the wisdom of grandmothers is greatly valued and many traditional healers—*sangomas*—are women. The training of a *sangoma* can last as long as seven years. A good *sangoma*—and Grace is among the best!—is expected to master the techniques of divination, the treatment of mental and physical disorders, plant and animal medicine use, ritual, chant and song, and soul ascension. Although Grace's mother was Zulu, her father's ancestry is Caribbean, so Grace's dialect is Afro-Caribbean in a sense and not strictly South African.

A lot of people have asked me if Martine and I are alike, and I'm quick to say that we're not. However, she and I do have one thing in common, and that's a passion for saving animals. I think a lot of kids feel that their pet is their friend, and that was definitely true of me. Like Martine, I often felt isolated or not as cool as everyone else. Although I did have lots of friends, my relationship with my black horse, Morning Star, was the most special of my childhood. I suppose I wrote *The White Giraffe* for anyone who understands what it's like to fall completely in love with an animal and have them love you back.

My hope for *The White Giraffe* is that it is as enjoyable to read as it was to write. If it encourages even one person to want to help wildlife or to visit or want to know more about Africa, that would make me incredibly happy.